"If Penelope's goal was to bring the hope that only Jesus can offer, please know she has been successful. She has this way of being able to authentically portray the human heart and all of its struggles that leaves one full of hope and love. That is not easily done—thank you. Excellent book. I loved it."

Mary Gliserman, Dean of Faculty, Vice-Principal, and teacher, The Daniel Academy associated with the International House of Prayer, Kansas City

"Penelope Wilcock has penned a wonderful medieval series. In *Remember Me*, she explores the struggle of a monk who has chosen his vocation wrongly to face the implications of his choice. The flavor of medieval and monastic life in Wilcock's work is to savor anew with each volume."

Mel Starr, author, *The Unquiet Bones, A Corpse at St. Andrew's Chapel,* and *A Trail of Ink*

"Magically beautiful, tender, and exquisitely drawn; full of teaching on love and forgiveness and almost every page brought a smile to my lips. I have fallen in love with all the books and I think Father William's journey, interlaced with Abbott John's is something of the best I have read."

Sue Ridley, Sussex, United Kingdom

6

The Hawk and the Dove

REMEMBER ME

A NOVEL

PENELOPE WILCOCK

::: CROSSWAY

WHEATON, ILLINOIS

Remember Me

Copyright © 2012 by Penelope Wilcock

Published by Crossway
   1300 Crescent Street
   Wheaton, Illinois 60187

Cover design: Amy Bristow

Cover image: Glenn Harrington, Shannon Associates

First printing 2012

Printed in the United States of America

ISBN-13: 978-1-4335-2663-3
ISBN-10: 1-4335-2663-8
PDF ISBN: 978-1-4335-2664-0
Mobipocket ISBN: 978-1-4335-2665-7
ePub ISBN: 978-1-4335-2666-4

Library of Congress Cataloging-in-Publication Data
Wilcock, Penelope.
 Remember me / Penelope Wilcock.
  p.　cm. (The hawk and the dove ; bk. 6)
 ISBN: 978-1-4335-2663-3 (tp)
 1. Monks—Fiction. 2. Monastic and religious life—History—Middle Ages, 600–1500—Fiction. 3. Religious fiction. I. Title.
PR6073.I394R46　　2012
823'.914—dc23　　　　　　　　　　2011041523

Crossway is a publishing ministry of Good News Publishers.

BP		21	20	19	18	17	16	15	14	13	12
14	13	12	11	10	9	8	7	6	5	4	3	2	1

FOR
ELVIRA McINTOSH

who never gave up searching for me
but went on until she found me
who lifted me up and encouraged me
who supported me as a writer—which is what I am
who understands Christ's call to community
and also to simplicity
and who looks for ways
to bring the Gospel to ordinary people
exactly as she finds them
and where they are.
God bless you, Elvira, and thank you.

REMEMBER ME

Jesus, remember me when you come into your kingdom
Jesus, remember me when you come into your kingdom
TAIZÉ CHANT OF THE WORDS OF THE THIEF ON THE CROSS

"Do this to remember me."
WORDS OF JESUS AT THE INSTITUTION OF THE EUCHARIST

If you find it in your heart to care for somebody else,
you will have succeeded.
MAYA ANGELOU

Some stories are true that never happened.
ELIE WIESEL

Dying is a wild night and a new road.
EMILY DICKINSON

Accept me, Lord, as thou hast promised,
and I shall truly live.
BENEDICTINE SUSCIPE

Can you not find it within you to
look with eyes of compassion?
TONY COLLINS

There is no fear in love.
1 JOHN 4:18

Contents

The Community of
St. Alcuin's Abbey

(Not all members are mentioned in *Remember Me*.)

Fully professed monks:

Abbot John Hazell	*once the abbey's infirmarian*
Father Chad	*prior*
Brother Ambrose	*cellarer*
Fr. Wm. de Bulmer	*cellarer's assistant (formerly an Augustinian prior)*
Father Theodore	*novice master*
Father Gilbert	*precentor*
Brother Clement	*overseer of the scriptorium*
Father Dominic	*guest master*
Brother Thomas	*abbot's esquire, also involved with the farm and building repairs*
Father Francis	*scribe*
Father Bernard	*sacristan*
Brother Martin	*porter*
Brother Thaddeus	*potter*
Brother Michael	*infirmarian*
Brother Damien	*helps in the infirmary*
Brother Cormac	*kitchener*
Brother Richard	*fraterer*
Brother Stephen	*oversees the abbey farm*
Brother Peter	*ostler*
Brother Josephus	*acted as esquire for Father Chad between abbots; now working in the abbey school*
Brother Germanus	*has worked on the farm, occupied in the wood yard and gardens*
Brother Mark	*too old for taxing occupation, but keeps the bees*
Brother Paulinus	*works in the kitchen garden and orchards*
Brother Prudentius	*now old, helps on the farm and in the kitchen garden and orchards*
Brother Fidelis	*now old, oversees the flower gardens*
Father James	*makes and mends robes, occasionally works in the scriptorium*
Brother Walafrid	*herbalist, oversees the brew house*
Brother Giles	*assists Brother Walafrid and works in the laundry*

Brother Basil	*old, assists the sacristan—ringing the bell for the office hours, etc.*

Fully professed monks now confined to the infirmary through frailty of old age:

Father Gerald	*once sacristan*
Brother Denis	*scribe*
Father Paul	*once precentor*
Brother Edward	*onetime infirmarian, now living in the infirmary but active enough to help there and occasionally attend Chapter and the daytime hours of worship*

Novices:

Brother Benedict	*assists in the infirmary*
Brother Boniface	*helps in the scriptorium*
Brother Cassian	*works in the school*
Brother Cedd	*helps in the scriptorium and when required in the robing room*
Brother Conradus	*assists in the kitchen*
Brother Felix	*helps Father Gilbert*
Brother Placidus	*helps on the farm*
Brother Robert	*assists in the pottery*

Members of the community mentioned in earlier stories and now deceased:

Abbot Gregory of the Resurrection	
Abbot Columba du Fayel (also known as Father Peregrine)	
Father Matthew	*novice master*
Brother Cyprian	*porter*
Father Aelred	*schoolmaster*
Father Lucanus	*novice master before Father Matthew*
Father Anselm	*once robe maker*

CHAPTER ONE

July

*L*ike a subtle wraith of mist in the still-dark of the night in late July he stole: silent and fleet, not hesitating. He came from the northwest corner of the church, where a small door led out into the abbey court from the side of the narthex. He did not cross the court, but passed stealthily along the walk between the yew hedge and the perimeter wall. Swift and noiseless he slipped along the close. It was a clear night but the dark of the moon, and only the stars gave light at this hour of the morning. At the end of Lauds, as the brothers shuffled back up the night stairs to resume their sleep, he had abstracted himself so unobtrusively that no one had seen. He had dodged back into the nave and stood in the deep shadows of the arcade in the side aisle on the north side of the church, hardly breathing. When all was still, he opened the small door with utmost caution; sliding the bolts back slowly and steadily without a sound, drawing the door closed and lifting and dropping the latch with barely a click, he left, and he was outside in the freshness of the night. Such faint light as the stars gave out found his silver hair, but that was the only glimmer of his presence as he slid from the abbey court along the close.

Peartree Cottage stood in the middle of the row of houses. The wicket gate stood ajar, and he pushed it open without a sound. As he stepped into the garden, the herbs gave up their fragrance underfoot. He felt a slug fall into his sandal. He stooped to flick out the slug and to scratch up a handful of earth that he flung at the upstairs window. No response. He tried again. This time the casement was opened with irritable vigor from the inside, and Madeleine's voice said sharply, "Who is it?"

Peering down suspiciously into the garden she might not have seen him, but he moved very slightly and most quietly spoke her name.

"Whatever do *you* want?" she whispered then, surprised.

"Will you let me in?" She heard the soft-spoken words. And as she came in the dark down the narrow ladder stairway, she realized the implications of this visit. Naturally cautious, she asked herself, *Are you sure you welcome this?* Just in going down the stairs, in opening the door, she realized her heart was saying, *Yes*.

As quietly as she could, she drew back the bolts and turned the key, lifted the latch, and opened the door to him.

"Whatever has possessed you? What on earth do you think you're doing?" she whispered fiercely as he came into the room. "Shall I light the candle?"

"Nay, nay! There are no curtains, you might as well light a beacon," he said softly. "Can you not see?"

He himself had good night vision; it was an honest question.

"I wouldn't need to see!" she whispered back. "Who else would risk us both being thrown out by coming here at this time of the night? Are you certain no one saw you?"

"It's only a fool who is ever certain no one saw him. I surely hope not though, or we are done for, as you say."

In silence they stood then, not three feet between them in the warm darkness of the cottage. Embers tidied together on the hearth still glowed from the small fire Madeleine had lit to cook her supper. They gave out hardly any light at all, but between the embers and the stars, the shapes of things in the room and the man who stood before her could be clearly enough discerned.

"Well?" she said then. "What should I think? Why are you here?"

He stood silently. She waited for his reply. She knew well enough but did not dare to presume what she hoped for.

"Do you . . . " His voice sounded unsure then; she heard the vulnerability in it. "Do you want me?"

Madeleine hesitated one last moment. There was still time to go back on this. She heard the intake of his breath in anxious uncertainty.

So she said in quick reassurance, "Of course I want you. With the whole of me. But is this honest? Isn't it stolen? Aren't we deceiving my brother?"

But he waited for no further discussion; she was in his embrace then, the ardent hold of yearning that she and he had waited for, it felt like for so long. He did not kiss her, simply held her to him, his body pressed trembling against hers.

She closed her eyes and took in the feel of him: the heat of his hunger for her, the beating of his heart and his quickened breath—all of him, bone and muscle and skin, the soul of him that lit every part, the pulse of desire and destiny. She loved the touch of him, the smell of him. She knew by heart every mannerism, every trick of movement and expression, every inflection of his voice. In any crowd she would have turned at his footstep, knowing whom she heard.

"I had to come to you," he whispered, his face against her hair. "I couldn't think, I couldn't sleep; I haven't been able to concentrate on anything. I know I can't have you, I do know. But I need to have the memory of just one time together for a refuge, for a viaticum—something real. I have been so desperate for you . . . to touch you . . . to hold you close to me . . . to feel your heartbeat and bury my face in your hair. Oh, my love, my love . . . I have *ached* to hold you."

She felt his hand lift to her head, caressing, and by the starlight she saw in his face such tenderness, such a flowing of love toward her as she had never imagined life might offer. He kissed her then, delicate kisses as light as a lacewing landing on a leaf: kissed her throat, her jaw, her cheekbones, her brow, kissed her eyelids closed, and then she felt his lips brush the curve of her cheek to find her mouth. He too closed his eyes as she parted her lips to the slow, beautiful, sensual rhapsody of his lover's kiss.

She felt the momentous tide of it overflow through all of her like the wave swell of the sea; then before she could bear to let him go, he drew back from his kiss, but still held her close. She wished she could see him properly, read the look in his eyes dark in the darkness.

"This is not what I thought," he whispered, "not what I expected."

He felt her body tense at his words and said hastily, "No! No, I didn't mean what you think. You are everything I want, all I long for! It's just that I had imagined this would lay things to rest—allow us to acknowledge something that is between us, and let it have its moment. I thought it might make it easier to relinquish it and give it back to God. But it doesn't feel like that now.

"Now that I am holding you I want never to have to let you go. I want us to share a bed and make love together, but I want us to share a home and make a life together, too. I want time to discover all the things I don't know about you yet. I want to watch you washing at the sink in the morning as the sun comes streaming in through the open door. I want to watch you brushing your hair. I want to find you kneading dough for our loaf at the table when I come in with the firewood for our hearth. I want you to teach me about herbs and how to grow them."

"Brother Walafrid could teach you about that," she murmured.

"Yes, I know," he whispered, "but I don't feel the same about Brother Walafrid as I do about you."

She had rested her head against the hollow beneath his collarbone as she listened to these words. She heard the smile in his voice, and he bent his head to kiss the top of hers.

"When I entered monastic life," he said, in the quietest undertone, "it was for pragmatic reasons—I had no money, was the thing, and that's what keeps me there still: no money. I've heard men talk about vocation often enough, but I couldn't feel my way to it—didn't really know what they meant. I have never had a sense of vocation until now.

"Now, all of me wants to be with all of you forever. Now I know what vocation is. But I am fifty years old, and I have no trade and no family. There is nothing I can offer you, and there is nowhere for us to go—even supposing you want me, too.

"You asked me if this was honest. It's probably the most honest thing I've ever done in my life. I know it's beyond reach. If I come back here again, someone will see, it will be discovered somehow—these things always are—but I thought I could risk just this one time. And I can offer nothing more. You and I both, we depend on the charity of the community to house us; there are no other choices. Like the poor everywhere, we have no rights and no options. But one night, for pity's sake, just *one night!* And it's not even a night, only a miserly hour between the night office and Prime. But after this, you must not watch for me nor wait for me, for I shall not be able to come to you—not ever again—but, oh my darling, remember me, remember this hour we had. If you get a chance of happiness with someone else, take it with both hands; I shall not be jealous. And deceiving John? Up to a point. I won't tell him, and I won't let him see. But I wouldn't lie to him, and I won't pursue this. It's just that I couldn't have lived the rest of my life starving to hold you for *one time* close to me. Maybe it is stolen. Yes—it is. But a starving man will snatch a crust of bread because it is life to him. And this is life to me."

He closed his eyes, drinking in the touch of her under his hands, the smell of herbs about her, the texture of her hair and her skin against his mouth, the softness of her body yielded against his. And then his mouth quested again for hers, and again he kissed her in deep, rapt communion. Like music, like a sunset, that kiss seemed to go on forever but had its own beginning and its end. And as he kissed her, William felt something change deep within him. He felt, from his belly, from his loins, from his heart, from his mouth, from his soul, the reality of what he was streaming forth unchecked, soul to soul. When their kiss found its conclusion, he realized that he had given all of himself, and it could never be taken back. Too late to choose a different path, to give less of himself or set any kind of boundary, he realized that this course he had chosen would break his heart. It was not realistic to suppose something like this could be contained in one night. When he slipped back through the half-light before the dawn, he would be leaving meaning and fulfillment and all his dreams behind.

He laid his cheek against her cheek, and their bodies melded together as if nothing could ever separate them; he tried to burn this moment so deep into his memory that no matter how much time passed it would never be erased again.

"When I first met you," said Madeleine then, moving her head to look at him as the first barely discernible beginnings of dawn lifted the dark, "I thought what a hard man you were— face like granite, eyes like flint I thought, no hope of give or take of any kind. But right in the middle of you there is this wellspring of such tenderness, isn't there? Something so delicate and gentle."

She saw the movement of his half smile, and the gray twilight delineated the beloved contours of his face.

"It used not to be the case," he said. "And even now, I think there might be only one soul in all the world who could find that upwelling and see it for what it is."

He kissed her mouth, so full and soft, and groaned with longing: "Oh God, I cannot let you go! I cannot give this back! Oh my sweet, my dearest—remember me. I shall live on this memory for the rest of my days. And if I ever find a way to you, if I can puzzle out any means for us to be together, I will come back for you. But do not wait, for that may never be. Truly, if you do find a chance of happiness with someone else, in heaven's name take it and that with my blessing. But even then, dearest, I beseech you—please—remember me."

And he enfolded her close, close against him, so that she felt the agonizing tenderness of his longing and his love. Then as the gray in the east lifted another shade toward light, knowing he must be back in the church before daybreak in time to mingle with the main ingress of brothers coming to prayers, he drew back from her, pressed his lips to her brow in one last kiss, and let himself silently out of the cottage with no further farewell.

"No . . . " she murmured, left standing by herself in the middle of the empty room, which never had felt lonely until now, "No . . . oh Jesu, mercy! Of your mercy, find us a way! Oh God have mercy! I cannot bear to lose this, too!"

Do not wait for me . . . he had said. Madeleine wondered whatever chance he thought there would likely be, for a woman of forty-three living on the charity of a monastery, to pick and choose a spouse. She knew that if this one chance with him was not given, she would never know the comfort and companionship of marriage at all. And she knew that even if by some miracle another suitor came her way, that could never be anything better than second best. She wanted *this* man: this complex, sardonic, guarded man with his complete disregard of rules, and his cool detachment, and the flame of absolute passionate tenderness that hid at the core of him.

The snatched hour had vanished more quickly than he could believe, and William left Madeleine's cottage later than he'd meant to. It had been his intention to return well before dawn and be in his stall in choir before any trace of sunrise colored the sky. His brothers coming down for the daybreak office would think—if they thought anything at all—that he had been unable to sleep and had come down early to win the first blessing and spend some time in private meditation. But already, as he latched the garden gate behind him, the stars were fading and the gray lifting every moment, tinged faintly with rose above the eastern rim of the hills. William felt the familiar contraction of anxiety in the hard muscles of his belly and his chest and his face. He could not afford to enter the chapel late, not for this morning office that offered no possibility of a man having been detained on the legitimate occupation of his daily duties.

Keeping close to the yew hedges, still blocks of darkness in the receding shadows of night, he skimmed noiselessly around the open spaces to the small door in the wall of the church that he'd left on the latch for his return. In a moment of panic he thought it had been locked, but steadying his hands to try the catch again, the second time it lifted properly; and he was inside, aware already of the distant but increasing rumbling reverberation of the community descending the night stairs in the clumsiness of waking recently and incompletely. He felt his heart thumping painfully as he disciplined himself to latching the door, sliding the bolts home, with the slowness of absolute silence.

Tension gripped him like a vise as he forced himself to walk soft and slow along the arcade of the side aisle, cursing himself for a fool as he heard the brothers already entering the choir from the night stairs that led down into the south transept. He felt his mouth go dry and his chest constrict as he slipped like a ghost across the north transept, trusting to the shadows to keep him hidden at this early hour. He had to hurry now. Going foxfoot along the narrow ambulatory that curved behind the high altar past the sacristy and little devotional shrines, he sped toward the south transept. He flattened himself against the cool stone of the wall, hardly breathing as the last of the brothers came down into chapel. Then he made himself wait for a slow count of ten, following the last man in from the general direction of the night stairs with all the flustered appearance of someone who has rolled late out of bed, just as the abbot gave the knock and the community rose for the cardinal office of Lauds.

The brothers were sleepy. Theodore, who sat opposite him in choir and occupied the cell next to him in the dorter upstairs, had a sharp eye for how things were with a man but was unlikely to take any notice of anyone fractionally late. William thanked God from the depth of his soul that he seemed to have gotten away with it. With difficulty he gave his attention to the psalm.

He was grateful, too, for the shelter of the Grand Silence extending beyond the chapel to the refectory as the brothers broke their fast, with bread and ale in these warmer months— they would have porridge to start the day once the frosts began.

As he stood in the frater with the others, keeping custody of his eyes, eating bread left over from yesterday with Brother Walafrid's ale—always more successful than his wines— William felt something in his soul clutch hungrily at the sense of peace and security in this house. They had allowed him in. They had accepted him. It was true that Abbot John's wise stricture against allowing too close an intimacy to develop between himself and William had hurt. William knew well that no personal attachments were permitted him and that the abbot's friendship must be for all of them in general and no one of them in particular, but he also knew the affection that had grown between himself and John was real. Severing it might be inevitable, but it was still painful. Even so, the dull ache of that faded into the background compared with the red-hot pain of renouncing Madeleine's company. He could not deny that John had been entirely right in insisting William visit her no more. As he chewed the bread and swallowed the ale, he reflected on what he had begun in going to her cottage and declaring his love. Until then, relinquishing her friend-ship had been the necessary sacrifice of a faithful monk. Its pain had felt intolerable, but the bitter taste had been sweet-ened by the upholding of his integrity. He had given up John; he had given up Madeleine—he had stayed faithful to this house and to the monastic way. The perpetual light of Christ's presence in the oratory of his heart's innermost chamber had burned on. It was different now. He had broken his vows. He had no claim on Madeleine nor hope of seeing her; he must make no claim on his superior but back off to the distance every brother must keep. All that was hard enough, but now he had thrown away his integrity as well.

He wiped his mouth on the napkin, his face morose. The security and peace of acceptance in this safe place had been besmirched and trampled on by his own deceit and by—he did not know what to call it—the thing that had taken place between him and Madeleine. He thought he should call it sin, but something in him, deeper than that framework of belief could touch, cried out against such a judgment. As he held her in his arms, as he kissed her, as he revisited the brief time they had shared and touched it again in memory while he sat in the frater now, chewing dry bread, all he could discern was the simplest, purest love. All he could feel was that he had been made to love her, born to love her. To call it temptation and sin fitted in with everything he'd always been taught, but it made no instinctive, intuitional sense at all.

In the Morrow Mass and at Chapter, he moved through the same grateful insulating cloaking of silence, glad of its protection.

After Terce, he went out into the abbey court and to the checker. Brother Ambrose came in after him, in cheerful mood.

"Overslept, did you?" he inquired, his tone playful. "The day rises still so early it's hard to be up with the lark!"

William lifted down the receipt book from its place on the shelf. He could see that he had set himself up for a whole tangle of lies and covert deception.

"It certainly is," he replied. "Did you pay the man for laying the hedge at St. Mary's graveyard, or hasn't he been for his money yet?"

He worked steadily then through the morning. It took him some time to discern the intended meaning of Brother Stephen's spelling on the chit from the farm, but eventually he managed to grasp that a saw had cost them tenpence and a hatchet ninepence ha'penny, and the smith would be calling to collect threepence ha'penny for mending something he couldn't read that seemed to have to do with a plow.

Conradus had asked for sieves to be mended and requested any cord they could spare for stringing herrings. It had cost him threepence to have some tankards bound and a guinea for several pots to be mended and bound. William frowned at the account. He hoped the novice hadn't been too zealous in his standards of improvement. He wondered how many pans it had been; Conradus hadn't made that clear.

He looked at the carpenter's and cooper's bills and the amount they had paid out to Jenny Tiler for the work her husband had done on the dovecote roof and wondered about the skills of the young men Theodore had in the novitiate. He thought they could do with a few more like Brother Thomas and rather fewer sensitive musical scholars in their next intake of postulants. It seemed ridiculous to him that they were now nearer forty than thirty monks living here in community and still paying someone else to tan the hide of the horse that died of colic after it broke into the feed store.

He accepted that clearing the ditches and scything the grass in the land they owned beyond the village was an inevitable expense. They couldn't be sending monks all that way over there to do the work, nor to make charcoal in the coppices. But surely they had enough pairs of hands for the work in their own farm and garden. And rabbits? "Upon my soul, this is extravagance!" he exclaimed aloud. "We have *paid* someone for rabbits? I must have words with our kitcheners about this; that won't do. It won't do at all. Have we no traps of our own?"

"It's Brother Cormac," explained Brother Ambrose. "He won't set traps."

"Won't set traps but he will buy rabbits, eh? Not anymore! I'll see him about it this afternoon."

He was as good as his word. After the midday meal he waited until the noise had subsided of the servers and kitcheners clearing tables and eating their own food and washing the pots from the meal. Then he went through to the kitchen where Brother Cormac and Brother Conradus were putting away the last few utensils to leave all the work surfaces uncluttered and clean.

"Brother Cormac," he said, "have you a moment?"

"For sure." Cormac gave the big bread bowl to Brother Conradus and came to hear what William had to say.

"Going through the accounts this morning, I see we've a recent item of rabbits purchased in the market."

Brother Cormac nodded. "For the guesthouse."

"Why are we buying rabbits? Up on the hill by the burial ground, up on the farm on the edges of the wood, are there not enough rabbits to supply our pot?"

Brother Cormac said nothing. He looked at the ground. He folded his arms self-protectively across his chest, his hands holding his upper arms. William waited, but no answer seemed forthcoming.

"Brother Ambrose says it is because you won't have traps set."

Cormac still neither looked up nor replied.

"For what possible reason can you justify buying rabbits from the market and not setting traps for our own? How do you think they caught the rabbits in the market?"

Cormac moved one hand to his brow. He looked as if he would have liked to obscure the whole of himself from William's scrutiny if he could.

"I know," he muttered. "I do know. We have rabbit because it's cheap, and they like to offer meat to the guests. If I asked for mutton, it would be more expensive, and you'd be asking me why we couldn't give them rabbit. But if we trapped them here . . . Oh, God, William—it would be me would have to set the traps!"

He took his hand away from his face then and stood, still hugging himself in protection, but his blue eyes looked straight into William's in appeal. "And even if you said you'd set the traps for me . . . Well . . . they scream when they are caught in the snare, and I couldn't . . . I just couldn't . . . Please—please can't we just buy them from the market?"

That blue gaze, seeing no answering recognition or compassion, dropped to the floor again.

William, exasperated, had actually opened his mouth to tell Cormac not to be so childish, when it was as though something in the depths of his heart moved in sudden protest. He stopped, surprised, and listened to his heart. Vividly, unexpectedly, he remembered Peregrine's face, everything exactly as it had been, at William's great refectory table in the days when he had been prior of St. Dunstan's. Peregrine, humiliated, cornered, reduced to complete vulnerability, while William pushed him further and further until he could bear no more. And William's heart said to him, *This is why people hated you.*

As the silence between the two men continued, Brother Conradus made himself as unobtrusive as he possibly could while he set about measuring out the ingredients for the pies they had planned for supper. He wondered if maybe he should just leave the pies for later and go away.

"What are we going to feed them, then, if we do not give them rabbit?" William asked. Brother Cormac looked up at him, the relief in his face more than William would have thought the situation warranted.

"Couldn't they eat fish, as we do? Or pigeons?"

"And if the guests clean us out of pigeons—I'm not being fanciful, we have a big influx at times—what do we eat?"

"Well . . . couldn't we eat beans . . . and eggs maybe . . . and cheese?"

William realized that he was not listening to a man who had given little thought to the matter; this came from the center of Cormac's heart.

"Brother Cormac," he said with a sigh, "you go on ordering your rabbits from the market. Do as you think best. Don't you worry."

As he turned and left the kitchen, and Cormac picked up a cloth to wipe down the table that was already clean, Brother Conradus kept his eyes focused firmly on his pastry, doing the best that he could to be there and yet not there at all.

William walked back to the checker, the encounter oddly clear and powerful in his heart. He felt as though his soul had become a battleground between faithfulness to the Christ who prioritized love above all else and the habits of cynicism and—he didn't like the idea but made himself face up to it—bullying, which he had always found worked well enough for him in the past. But if the Christ who prioritized love was the Lord of this community and the Lord of his own life, what he couldn't disentangle was where his feelings for Madeleine fitted in. He thought the only way he could cope with shutting her out of his mind would be if he barred the way to every impulse of tenderness and humanity, reverting to the arid state he'd been used to before he came here. The more he went on thinking about it, the more clearly he realized that was no longer an option for him. His heart had been broken open to life and love, and he didn't think he could seal it up again, even if he wanted to. And, he had to admit in the still small voice of his innermost being, he *didn't* want to, not when it came to it. And he thought that might be his salvation, but it was not unconnected with being in love.

This was not the first time in his life that William had used account books as a refuge from thinking about things that threatened and confused him.

"Any joy with Brother Cormac?" Brother Ambrose asked him cheerily as he walked through the door.

"I said he could go on ordering the rabbits from the market." Brother Ambrose had to strain to hear him, and William did not look at him.

"Oh. I see." Ambrose thought it wisest to withdraw from further discussion of the matter. "Never mind," he said sympathetically. "We all have that trouble with Brother Cormac."

William did not reply. He sat down at his table and picked up the next scrap of parchment from the pile of notes jotted down by the brothers, and receipts and bills from tradesmen. He looked at it in bafflement. He simply couldn't read this monk's handwriting at all.

✠   ✠   ✠

"I would speak with thy cellarer." Old Mother Cottingham accosted Brother Martin on his way back to the gatehouse after the midday meal.

"Brother Ambrose?" He regarded her with kindly amusement, this diminutive ancient lady, bent and leaning on her gnarled stick, her wild gray hair in disarray, her shawl awry, only a few teeth left in her jaw, but her eyes as bright and sharp as ever. Eyes that saw everything—on the inside as well as the outside. There was nothing wrong with her hearing either, remarkably.

"Nay, not Brother Ambrose. The other one. Lean, wiry fellow with a swift step; hard, sallow face, and silver hair. Him."

Brother Martin grasped whom she had in mind.

"He should be over at the checker this afternoon, good mother. You should feel free to speak to him there."

Mother Cottingham stood up as straight as she could, the better to look Brother Martin uncompromisingly in the eye. "I don't want to speak to him at the checker," she said. "I want to speak to him alone, and I want him to call at my cottage. Will tha ask him for me?"

Brother Martin could think of no reason why not. Mother Cottingham, who must have seen eighty years a while back and stopped counting, presented no danger of either temptation or scandal. She had lived there from time immemorial. Her husband, knowing his days numbered, had secured her a dwelling in the safety of the abbey ground during the early days of Abbot Gregory's time. Father Peregrine, who disliked the selling of corrodies and thought the abbey was best inhabited by the monks (and nobody else), had left the cottages empty when their residents died. Father Chad had filled them again, to raise funds urgently needed, after Peregrine had become too ill to contemplate any realistic prospect of resuming office. But whether the cottages in the row stood filled or empty, Mother Cottingham stayed put in her house, the fifth in the row, next door neighbor to Peartree Cottage. She was not thought to be poor, for she gave generously to the abbey coffers and did not depend on the community for her daily necessities; it was only the house and the proximity to the brothers that her husband had wanted to provide, for they'd had no family beside each other, and he would not think of her all alone in the world after his death. The brothers knew nothing of her earlier history; there remained not one of them now who remembered Ellen

Cottingham as a laughing young woman, the beauty of the village and the apple of her husband's eye. There was no one left who recalled the griefs she had lived through: bearing four sons, three of them dying one after another as babes and her firstborn taken with lockjaw at nineteen years old—a swift and hideous death. She had gone almost mad with grief for her lads, and her man who loved her so had grieved over her grieving. It had taken a long time, but somewhere in midlife she had finally made her peace with God, and she became very devout. St. Alcuin's grew to be home from home for her. Simon Cottingham knew she would be all right without him if he could leave her a little nest under the eaves of the abbey church, and he had gone to his rest in peace when it had been finally arranged. Whatever else he had to bequeath her was long forgotten; her affairs were managed by a lawyer in York, but she seemed to have enough to get by.

"Yes, I can ask him." Brother Martin smiled at her. "Urgently, do you mean? What shall I say it's about?"

"Nay, nothing that cannot wait until tomorrow," the old crone replied. "I wanted to make a little gift to the abbey is all."

Brother Martin laughed. "That should fetch him quick and make him happy—and there's not much does; he isn't the most cheerful soul on any day of the week. Yes, I'll tell him for you, Mother, never fret."

"Thank 'ee kindly, tha's a good lad." And Mother Cottingham made her slow, creaking passage back to her cottage. She saw no sign of her neighbor as she hobbled slowly by, for Madeleine had gone out to take her goat to new pasture and then had a visit to make to a newly delivered mother in the village.

Brother Martin proved faithful in his errand, and William, being not behind with any matters needing his attention, had time that same afternoon to visit Mother Cottingham in her home.

He walked briskly along the close without even turning

his head to look at Madeleine's cottage—which did not mean he didn't see it and note the closed air that signaled she was out—he just didn't turn his head. Mortifying the eyes while still noticing everything was an impossibility that had been required of him from his first days under novitiate discipline. It no longer seemed difficult now.

Mother Cottingham's house looked as neat and trim as any in the row. He had instigated a program of repairs himself, to be done once the harvests were in, but before that Brother Ambrose had been conscientious in his duties and looked after the buildings well. Inside was another matter—what happened indoors was the responsibility of each tenant. Mother Cottingham could no longer manage the housework she might once have done, and he knew from his visits to check for repairs needed that her home was grimier than it could have been, but not too bad. Even so, he did not especially look forward to this call. He tapped on the cottage door and waited respectfully to be invited in. It took the old woman a long time to answer his knock, as he knew it would, but still he waited because that was what she preferred. He noticed as he stood there patiently that her garden had been weeded.

When at last she opened the door to him, he saw that the room inside looked cleaner and brighter than last time he'd been in it. The floor had been swept and the ledges dusted, the pewterware scoured bright, and the pots set neat on the shelf. Momentarily puzzled, he quickly concluded that the difference between now and his previous visit was that Madeleine had moved in next door. Evidently she had spread a sheltering wing over her aged neighbor, and perhaps it gave her some comfort and filled a void somewhere, for she had loved her mother and so suddenly lost her.

"Come in, lad. Come in and sit thee down."

William could think of a hundred and one things he'd rather be doing than whiling away the afternoon in what threatened to be an extended visit. He was on the verge of saying he wouldn't sit down because he couldn't stay long, when he remembered Abbot John counseling him earlier in the spring to take the love that ached in his heart for Madeleine and lavish it on those who needed it and otherwise had nobody to love them. He had admired this line of thinking but had so far ignored the advice. With the wound of grief at what he had done Thursday night still open and wet in his soul—the agony of parting from Madeleine forever sent him dizzy with sorrow if he let his mind dwell on it—he thought this might be a good time to allow the love that still overflowed inside him to be channeled in a direction where it might do some good.

"Thank you, my lady," he said therefore, with the gentle courtesy of a knight addressing a queen. Ellen's sharp glance searched for cynicism or mockery, it being her experience that old women are usually treated more patronizingly than that by such middle-aged men as notice them at all, but she saw none on his face. She saw sadness though, the fine-drawn skein of suffering indefinably incorporated and revealed in his features.

"Tha looks unhappy. Art tha unhappy?" she asked him bluntly. She had found that though old age brings little to recommend it, one of its few privileges was the advantage of being indulged in speaking her mind. She had given up trying to please others in her late seventies, and nothing caused her to miss the habit or experience the slightest twinge of regret at its cessation.

She regarded William calmly; he looked lost for words. It was not the monastic way for the brothers to discuss personal matters with anyone outside the community, and she saw that her question embarrassed him a little. That did not trouble her. She loved the abbey, and she loved God, but she did not feel bound herself by the customs of monastic tradition.

Mother Cottingham had two chairs, old and beautifully crafted, set to either side of an equally old cherrywood table.

Moving slowly from the door, she took her seat in one chair and gestured that he should take the other. Grateful for an escape from her initial scrutiny, he was glad to make a task of its own out of thanking her and sitting down.

"I have a small gift to make to the abbey," she began, and he murmured his thanks.

"Why art tha not happy?" she persisted unexpectedly. William hesitated, then decided to go for evasion.

"But, madam, we are more grateful than I can say for your gifts to us. Your kindness is neither expected nor looked for; even so, it means a lot and is always appreciated. I should not wish you to think I am not pleased at your gift—I value it immensely."

"I'm sure tha does. Thy unhappiness has nothing to do with me and mine; it's all thy own. Why art tha not happy?"

Unaccustomed to finding himself caught on the back foot in this manner, William regarded her mutely for a moment, then dropped his gaze. It crossed his mind that he had traveled further than he might ever have imagined from the suave, assured, indifferent man he used to be.

"No matter," the old woman continued. "Tha doesn't want to tell me. But I do see."

Startled by the assurance and meaning in her tone, William looked up at her again. Her gaze, bright eyed and unwavering, met his.

"I want to give thee five shillings for the work of the abbey," she said.

His eyebrows rose. "Are you sure? That's as much as a month's rent for a farm!"

"Aye, I know," she said serenely, "and it's what I want to give."

"That's very generous, Mother Cottingham. It will be a great help to us . . . if . . . if you're sure it will not leave you short."

"I have it here; there's the bag—take it. I can spare it. And then, Brother Cellarer, I also have a question for thee."

He drew the purse of money toward him with a quiet repetition of his thanks as her wrinkled and age-freckled hand, misshapen with rheumatism, pushed it across for him to take. But he let the bag lie on the table while he waited to hear what she had to ask.

"I would like to know, Brother Cellarer, what tha was doing leaving Mistress Hazell's house before sunup this last Thursday and stealing so silent away along the close."

William felt his heart, his chest, his throat constrict. Mother Ellen watched the slow flush of color in his face. His eyes, pale lamps, intelligent, met hers. He did not speak. Nor did she. She waited, the alert surveillance of her small eyes giving no quarter as she observed his consternation. He dropped his gaze to his hand as his fingertip traced a knot of wood in the polished top of the table.

"What you saw," he said at last, quietly, "is what you thought you saw. I was doing what you think I was doing. Except, you should know this . . . " He glanced up at her; serious, earnest, she thought. "Whatever you may be assuming, I want you to know: what you saw was not the usual caricature of a lusty monk stealing forbidden goods in the bed of an easy woman. I love Madeleine. I love her with everything in me. I did her no dishonor, nor would I ever. What should be saved for marriage will remain so. But it was indeed for love that I came to see her."

Mother Cottingham weighed these words. William, waiting for her reply, noted his own responses of tension, fear, and foreboding twitching along every muscle. He felt sick.

"But tha art a monk," she said simply.

He nodded soberly. "Well, and here's the difficulty of it: before I am a monk, I am a man. And in trying to hold the two together I have failed completely. I am clothed. I am vowed. I am professed. I am committed. And still I have fallen utterly, hopelessly in love. Madam, I do not need you to point out to me there is an inconsistency; I am racked on it every hour of every day. My abbot had seen the way my heart was tugging, and he has forbidden me to see Madeleine or speak to her, and very wisely too. So I have kept away, until last Thursday, when I could no longer bear the longing or suffer being parted from her anymore. I thought if I came to her, I could explain why I had stayed away, I could hold her in my arms just the one time and make a clean break of it, and the thing would be done. But I never thought anything could be so painful as this has turned out to be."

She watched his face, miserable as he considered his options, which seemed devastatingly few and bleak. He toyed absently, unseeing, with the twisted strings of the linen money bag. Then at last he raised his eyes to meet hers.

"I have no right to do this, but I am begging you not to tell my abbot. I fully realize that will implicate you in my deceit and in my sin, but . . . oh God . . . if you knew how this has felt . . . I have given my word to Madeleine that I will not go to her again. It was only for once. And I pray I may have the strength to keep to what I said. Although . . . " With a gesture of hopelessness, he waved his hand in dismissal and looked away from her eyes again. "I can see no hope . . . no light . . . ." He shook his head, despairing. "But I will try to be faithful. I promise you I will. It's my misfortune you were awake to watch me stumble and fall. Mother, if this becomes known, Madeleine will lose her home here, and I will be turned out. And I . . . it's complicated . . . the world outside here is not a safe place for me to be."

She watched his misery, the haggard lines of his face, the tremor in his hands.

"You are asking me to lie for thee?"

He shook his head. "If it comes to that—no. Only to keep close the truth you know."

He swallowed. "Please. Please. I am begging you. I cannot

take care of her. I cannot provide for her. We have nowhere to go."

"Tell me," said Mother Cottingham, "are all the monks in this abbey like thee? Are they none of them what they seem?"

Again he shook his head. "Nay; they are not—not like me, I mean. In every community there will be men who have their secrets, their liaisons, their clandestine passions and hidden griefs. But that said, this house is a place of integrity. Where I was before, every man in the priory was like me. And the villagers burned the place down. You have met Father Oswald? He escaped with me. I dodged the rough justice better than he did, but our refuge is here."

Mother Ellen considered him, then she made up her mind.

"Thy secret will be safe with me, child. But there are conditions to my silence."

There would be. There always were.

His sense of relief at her promise of discretion was substantially diminished by his apprehension about the demands she might seize her chance to make. William had never imagined himself becoming vulnerable to blackmail, but he saw that was exactly what he'd done.

Child, she had called him. He wondered how old she was, this ancient hag, to think of a man of fifty as a child. He thought of the age of time that must pass before he reached the fullness of years she had now and realized he had set himself to trudging that road one weary step at a time, with nothing but the memory of a furtive, stolen hour to keep him going. The reflection opened in him an awareness of a reservoir of grief so black and wide and so impossibly deep it could never be fathomed or contained. It must overwhelm him, and for a moment it almost did.

But he recollected himself, recalling that all of us think principally of ourselves, and he did not delude himself that his private agony would be the first thing on Mother Cottingham's mind. She had a deal to strike. She wanted something out of this. This withered old woman was of an age to be his mother, and William's memories of childhood recollected neither clemency nor understanding; he was not expecting either to be offered him now.

"I imagined it would be so," he responded, addressing himself with an effort to her talk of conditions to be met. "Well?"

"Tha hast no idea what tha's looking at, not at all, hast tha? Tha thinks, 'spiteful old crone, gossip and hunger for power.' But tha's wrong. Look again, for I'm not what tha sees. Still alive in me is a girl crazy with love, her heart beating like a drum, full of longing, full of life. There's the wild tearing of sorrow as I laid the last of my infants in the ground, and then my son, the only one that lived, snatched from me still a boy in his twentieth year. I am not only what's given to thy eyes to see, Brother Cellarer. As tha'rt a monk but tha'rt also a man, so I'm a crone, withered and half-dead—but I'm a woman, and I remember. I remember the look in thy eyes today, for I've seen it before. I know the longing, and I know the sorrow. I don't want to keep thee on a string or wring thy heart fiercer than the pain that's wringing it now. Only this I am asking—wilt tha promise me, lad? When I lie dying, I would have it be thee that brings me the Viaticum and says the prayers for my soul. And between that day and this, I would have thee be my confessor. Those are my conditions. If tha wilt do that for me, I'll keep silence for thee."

This struck William as so very unlikely that he could find no immediate reply. The idea that anybody who knew anything about his personal history, from his childhood up to the present hour of the present day, could place into his priestly hands the care of their soul struck him as incongruous in the extreme.

"Couldn't you find somebody more faithful? I should have thought you could choose any brother at random in this abbey, starting with the newest postulant and going all the way up to the abbot, and you couldn't help but pick a more virtuous soul than mine."

Ellen Cottingham listened to the bitterness and the incredulity in his voice. "I doubt I'd find one more human," she said, "and that's why I'm asking thee. Because I am human, too. Tha gives me hope."

Not that many things in life surprised William, but those words did. She watched the amusement glimmer in his face. "'Human'?" he said. "Well, yes, I'm that. 'Hope'—of that I'm not sure."

He glanced at her. "If you can cope with the humanity and manage without the hope, yes, I'll gladly be your confessor."

She nodded. "That will do me well. So this is why tha'rt unhappy then. When I used to see thee about the place before, helping Madeleine, tha looked different. I don't think tha saw me, but I often saw thee. And I liked the look of thee. Thy face was all laughter."

She watched his eyes, remembering, the recollection of those times passing across his soul like the shadow and light of clouds under sunshine passing across the moor.

"I had several weeks of purest joy," he said. "Two things happened to me. The first was that, after something our abbot said to me, I prayed to the Lord Christ asking him if he would forgive my sins and come to abide in my heart—make himself real to me. And this he did. It was just at sunrise, and the room flooded with glory, and my heart flooded with glory, too. It was sunrise in my soul as well. I was alight with joy. I would never have believed it possible to contain so much joy without some kind of explosion. I walked on light after that—well, things went on as normal, and I don't know that I looked all that different, but inside I felt like a new creation.

"Then on the tail of that I found myself falling in love with Madeleine. I heartily disliked her when first we met; she had been badly shocked and hurt and was full of the anger of grief, and an unkindness in some of the things she said offended me. But as soon as I got to know her better, I saw who she really was and . . . oh, it was gradual, not immediate. But there came a day when I realized she was the first thing on my mind when I woke up and the last when I fell asleep, and I couldn't get through a day without finding some reason to call at Peartree Cottage. And my abbot rightly put a stop to that. It was in the last days of Eastertide that I beseeched the Lord Jesus to make my heart his dwelling place. It was in the fourth week after Trinity that my abbot said I must never go near Madeleine again. And I lost all the joy. It was as though the sun went out.

"In those days between, I was so happy. I never knew what happiness was before that. I entered monastic life because I could see no other realistic options, and it suited me well enough. I was a shrewd obedientiary but a bad monk. Before I came here, I got on well enough; didn't give a toss what anyone thought, and lived as I pleased for my own advantage and the advantage of my priory—I was the prior. But here they made me see things—and see myself—differently. I've spent most of the time feeling bitterly ashamed of myself and working my fingers to the bone trying to repay their goodness to me. I was supposed to be a reformed character, and that was going well until I fell in love. The joy of Christ's presence in your heart is one thing; the love of a woman is another. Obviously. For a monk."

Ellen listened, enthralled, to this account. The brothers of St. Alcuin were friendly and pleasant, but they did not confide in lay folk their passions and struggles. The boundaries were courteously but absolutely maintained. Such an insight as this was not something that had ever come her way before. She was fascinated, and as he stopped talking, lapsing into stillness, his eyes hopeless and his face drawn, she watched the small movements of thoughts in his countenance, and she held this encounter to be a privilege, and an honor. She realized that he could not have this conversation with any of his brothers, not even his abbot who must not know he had come back to see Madeleine again. It occurred to her that she had become his confessor before he had become hers. An old woman in any society is redundant and invisible; that made the gift of his honesty and self-revelation especially precious to Ellen. She would never betray him—nor Madeleine, who had been kind to her, sweetened her life with her company, and done a hundred little tasks and errands for her that seemed to be getting harder for her to accomplish every day.

"Is the joy of Christ's presence with thee all extinguished by this parting?" she asked him.

He hung his head, ashamed. "Yes," he whispered. "It is."

Ellen was grateful she still had sharp ears. It occurred to her you would need good hearing to be a confessor.

"Can tha not find him still, in thy heart? Is he not still there?"

She asked for her own curiosity as much as to help him.

William looked at her. Tears glittered in his eyes. "Oh, he is there. My heart is become like a bloody torture chamber. He hangs on his cross and groans and shifts his weight and sweats and weeps and waits to die. Yes, he is with me. But he is no ray of sunshine now."

He was trembling. He took his hands from the tabletop and put them in his lap, inside the wide sleeves of his habit.

"Sounds as though tha'rt very lonely," said Ellen.

He nodded, mutely. She watched him strive for mastery over himself, and her soul saluted his strength as he achieved it.

"I have always been a solitary man," he said then. "I had little regard for the human race and little desire for human company. But I've changed. Since Christ brought me here and broke me open, things have been different with me. There is such real, living fellowship among the brothers here. And I value my abbot's good opinion. I love him. But all that is wrecked now. I am back to covert ways, hiding my heart and trying not to seem what I am." He stopped, abruptly. "Yes, it feels lonely." His final admission was barely audible.

"Tha'rt a good man, though," she said.

Hunched in misery, he shook his head. "No. I am not."

"Yes, tha'rt a good man. Tha's proved it to me."

He raised his head to look at her, frowning in puzzlement.

"Tha hasn't seen what I've offered thee, in asking thee to be my confessor, hast tha, Brother Cellarer?"

He looked blank. "No. Well—apart from your undeserved confidence in me, and the honor that such a request always is, both of which are very gracious of you. And by the way, I am not the cellarer—and do you not know my name?"

"We are suffered here in the cottages because we have bought the right to be here. But we are not admitted to any kind of closeness with the brethren. I think thy name might be William, because I have heard Madeleine say it, and the way she said it makes me think she must have been talking to thee; otherwise I would not have known it."

"Yes. I'm William. And it's Father William because I am a priest, and without that I could not be your confessor. But plain William will do fine."

"Well, Father William, I know tha'rt a good man and a good monk, because tha's said yes to shepherding my soul only because I asked thee—and to buy my silence maybe. But tha sees, does tha not, I am an old woman, halt and frail. I would hope tha would do me the kindness of coming to my little cottage to hear my confession, not make me come all the way across to the church. It would not be so often—every few weeks. Maybe after Vespers, when tha's had thy supper and the day's work is done. When the light goes off the day and the dusk brings the shadows. The gardens at the back of our cottages are but one long strip, really. The dividing walls are low."

William looked at her, the implication of what she was saying slowly sinking in, and he began to laugh.

"Oh, Mother Cottingham! God bless you—you are a woman after my own heart! What a thoroughly rascally scheme! By my faith, you would have made a good archdeacon! Oh, I am tempted, sorely tempted! But it will not do. See, I really love Madeleine; this is not a dalliance. And I love Abbot John, too—besides which, John is no fool and he walks a straight line. He would not be long in feeling his way to the truth of it. And I would be stripped of my tunic and flogged in Chapter and flung out to find what way I could in the world—and Madeleine would follow after. She needs security, Mother. She needs a proper home. It would be no true love to take that away from her. We are not young enough; the years of learning a trade and building a life have gone. I must stand by what I have set myself to do. And I cannot bear the thought of passing her on my way here, 'Good morrow, Mistress Hazell,' as if I barely knew her. But thank you—thank you, thank you—for being on our side and trying to make a way through for us. It means a lot. God bless you. There. That's one outrageous, naughty sin forgiven. What else have you got hidden in your heart?"

"Eh—it's good to see tha can laugh! I was beginning to wonder. I have no more sins for thee, child. I've the time but not the inclination at the age I am. No doubt tha can lead me astray and give me something to confess. Work thy way along the whole row, mayhap—why stop at Madeleine and me? Anyway, get thee gone. I thank thee for thy courtesy in coming to see me; that goes a long way for an old woman. Tha'll find when tha grows old, folk don't go out of their way for thee anymore. Tha'll become invisible too, of no regard anymore. And I am grateful to thee. Tha came promptly, and tha spoke to me as if I were a duchess. Here's thy money for the abbey then. God bless thee, and remember this door stands always open to thee."

He stood to go. "Stay where you are, Mother—don't get up,

there's no need." He hesitated, then leaned over the table and left a light kiss on her brow. "Thank you for keeping our secret." Then he took up the money bag and, bowing to her in courtesy, turned and let himself out of the cottage.

Mother Cottingham stayed in her chair, just sitting quietly. She thought about Father William, her confessor now, and savored the memory of the look on his face as he left her cottage. She had not been able to lift his troubles away from his shoulders and carry them for him, but she could see that he had felt comforted. She thought of Madeleine and admired her discretion. Not by the smallest hint had Madeleine ever indicated that she might have any sort of connection of friendship with one of the brothers. Ellen thought about the two of them. She cupped her arthritic, old hands in her lap, and in her imagination she held the two of them there together . . . and she prayed for them. She prayed for a happy ending to their story. She prayed that God who made them would understand . . . that he would not be severe with them . . . that he would have mercy on their humanity. And then, just as she was beginning to doze off to sleep in the warmth of the afternoon, she had an idea.

Chapter
Two

August

John did not find the responsibility of the abbot's chapter and the homilies at Mass easy to carry. Years in the infirmary had accustomed him to the idea that all anyone needed to hear him say were things along the lines of "Drink it all. No, all of it. No, you really must." Or, "Roll over then—there, that's it. Just hold steady, exactly as you are. Nearly finished."

He took to the work of administration and pastoral listening with almost no adjustment, but the concept of the community attending diligently to his theological ruminations struck him as somewhere between laughable and terrifying. He prepared carefully and dug deep. He knew that St. Alcuin's housed scholars of far higher caliber than his, so usually what he offered them were his reflections on many years of walking the monastic way, the memories and experiences that had acted as shafts of light for him in his own struggles to be faithful to the Christ he loved.

Today he wanted to talk to them about the Eucharist, principally because Father Theodore had asked him to. The novices were discussing the theology of the Eucharist in their morning studies.

"Theodore, are you having me on? Your knowledge of Eucharistic theology is so far ahead of anything I have to say, it's completely out of sight! What more could they possibly need to learn from me?"

Theodore smiled. "Thank you, Father, for the compliment. I teach them what's in the books and the sermons. I tell them what the holy Church has laid down and show them the Scriptures and make them read the works of the church fathers. But what I was really hoping is that you could speak to them out of your life. Show them what the Eucharist can mean to an ordinary monk trying to get on from day to day with his brothers, as well as to a great mind with a following of disciples."

A strange silence followed these words. "Oh, holy saints!" Theodore exclaimed, horrified. "You didn't think—I don't mean *my* great mind and the disciples in our novitiate! I meant like Jerome and Augustine with their following of young men gathered around them!"

John fiddled with the knotted cord of the rope belting his habit as he thought about this. "The trouble is, Theo, I never really paid attention. I don't think I even realized they *had* gatherings of disciples. I was always more interested in the practical side of things—what works, what makes people better, what keeps them sane and well."

"Yes." Theodore smiled at him. "That's what I was hoping for."

So John got his homily ready for Mass, feeling only a bit of a fraud while the community waited respectfully on his pronouncements concerning the holy Eucharist.

"'Remember me,'" he said, "is what Jesus asked of us. 'Do this to remember me.' We think about remembering as looking back on times past, a nostalgic recollection of something that has gone now. But remember is also the opposite of dismember. When something has been broken apart, dismembered, we look at the broken pieces and remember how it used to be, and put it back together, make it whole again.

"I've done a lot of that in the infirmary. People have come

to me with an abscess or a runny eye or a rash, asking if I have anything that can make them better. And I did the best I knew to make each one into the man he used to be, bringing him back to full health, if I could.

"The heart of illness is imbalance. Things out of balance go wrong very quickly—that's why we have to keep the discipline of rest and recreation as well as work and prayer, eating and enjoying ourselves as well as fasting and disciplining ourselves. You have to get the balance right.

"And the Eucharist heals us. So what has intrigued me about it has been trying to see how and what it was balancing, that it can be such a healing thing.

"Now, you probably recall, from your studies of St. Augustine—um . . . the African one—that he taught his cat-echumens, when they received the bread, the host of the Eucharist, to respond to the words 'The body of Christ' by saying 'Amen,' as we all do. But he told them, 'Let your *Amen* be for *I am.*'

"See? '*I am* the body of Christ.' That's . . . quite momentous. But it's true enough. We—you, me, all of us together—we are the body of Christ.

"So let's think about this a bit. Jesus, at the Last Supper, when he tore the bread to pieces, said to his disciples, 'This is my body, broken for you. Do this to remember me.'

"Do what? Not just consecrate bread and wine, eat and drink, as he did; I think he meant more than that. I think he meant that we should gather as they did, that we should share as they did, that we should hold together and walk the way in faithfulness as they did, eat together, pray together, discuss together.

"But of course, as soon as we do this, what do we notice? Before very long it becomes apparent to us that this bunch of brothers is immensely annoying. You sit in silent meditation and the man next to you keeps holding his breath and then letting it go in a sigh—every couple of minutes, until you think 'Oh, shut up, you idiot! Just *breathe normally!*' You sit at the meal table and try to focus on the reading from the martyrology as you've been told, but you can't because the brother beside you is bashing his dish so vigorously as he scrapes out his pottage that you can't hear what the reader is saying, and you think, 'Jesus, Mary, and Joseph—what's the matter with you, man? Do it *quietly!*' And then you sit down in your stall at Vespers, and you have this little tickle in your throat that makes you keep clearing it, and you're trying to be discreet, but you suddenly catch the eye of the man opposite you, and you think 'What? What's his problem? I'm doing my *best!*'

"Living in community isn't easy, especially when the only material for the job is us lot.

"There are people we can't stand the sight of, men we're afraid of, brothers we're frankly jealous of, and some who make us feel so inadequate we wonder if the place wouldn't be better off without us.

"The body of Christ—yes, we may be; broken, we certainly are. And we may be limping along to begin with, but when Christ takes us into his hands he breaks us again—tears us to shreds at times. He has to grab hold of our pride . . . arrogance . . . contempt . . . cynicism . . . hardheartedness . . . . He has to break those things up, or there would never be any humility, no compassion, no gratitude.

"So the body of Christ is broken—in the bread, on the cross, and in the community; it's dismembered, it isn't well. That word 'well'—it's an old word, and it means the same as 'whole.'

"And what Jesus is saying—at least, I think this is what he's saying—is that as we gather together like this, suffer him to break us like this, then Christ, who has been dis-membered in crucifixion and in sin, is re-membered in our gathering, made whole in our community, in our communion. Comm-union, comm-unity: they mean being as one together, being reconciled in a fellowship of humility and forgiveness. The brokenness of his body (and we *are* his body) is healed in our love, in our common life—which is his love, his life, in us.

"So—do you see? There is a balance. We are made whole in Christ, but also—I hardly dare to say it—Christ is made whole in us.

"When we refuse to love and accept one another, when we break the communion of love, we dismember the body of Christ. When we come here in the Mass, embrace each other humbly and honestly in the kiss of peace, kneel in humility to receive Christ's body in the host, a miracle of healing happens. When the brokenness of Christ's body touches the brokenness of our souls, the blood of his love flows from one to the other, mingling our life with his. We become one body, one blood with Him. We are accepted. We are forgiven. We are healed.

"It's about maintaining a state of balance in the community as a body—like breathing in and breathing out—the humility to receive from him and the generosity to give of ourselves. Wellness can happen because life balances for healing again as we remember him."

Brother Robert, probably the least promising of Theodore's novices, listened to this, rapt. He had absolutely no idea what his abbot was talking about, but he liked Father John. He sensed his kindness, and his strength. In the short time he'd been in the novitiate he had watched his abbot battered to his knees by grief and distress, and watched him get up again and carry on. He thought Father John probably knew what it meant to be broken.

In the silence for reflection the abbot left before they moved on, Brother Robert looked at the faces of his brethren in community. Father Theodore, his face gentle and still, sat with his eyes closed. Brother Thomas was evidently bothered by a splinter in his thumb, which he was trying to get out. The abbot himself sat with eyes downcast, motionless, his hands folded into his sleeves. Brother Robert's eye lighted on the cellarer—or was he the cellarer? Wasn't Brother Ambrose the cellarer? Anyway, the man who had come to the community just a few months back during Lent. Father William. Intrigued, Robert looked at the tense, hard lines of his face: composed, yes. Peaceful? Not at all. He gave the impression of simply enduring being alive, and Brother Robert wondered why. Wasn't he happy here?

How do people know when someone is watching them? William glanced up quickly, straight into Robert's eyes, and for a moment the young man felt suddenly frightened, for no real reason at all, just the look in William's eyes, which scared him. And then the community stood for the *Credo*.

The Eucharist was the heart and soul of the way these men had chosen, and it sat as a central jewel within the setting of the monastic hours. Lauds and Vespers, the cardinal offices (named after *cardo*, the word for a hinge), opened and closed the central working hours of the day. Compline folded their tired minds and bodies under the wing of God's silence at bedtime. The night office was the mysterious trysting hour that kept watch with the God who neither slumbers nor sleeps. The offices of Sext and None reminded them that they took their meal only after they had prayed, and that the work of their lives was their focus on God, not the occupation of their hands in their various tasks—those must be set aside when they heard the bell ring for the Office, however pressing or absorbing the task had become.

And beyond the rhythm of the monastic hours was the private prayer of each man, the moments in which his heart became the hallowed ground where he tasted the Love beyond all loves that he had sworn to serve—sometimes bitter, sometimes sweet, sometimes full of dread like an ember that threatened to scar and sear his soul, occasionally blissful, sometimes a time of tears and seeing his own shame.

Every one of them knew that prayer would be the lifeblood

of the way he had set himself to walk; without it his heart would wither and his soul would die.

So on the other side of the choir from the Lady Chapel, the south side, an inconspicuous door led into a small oratory for private prayer—a simple, quiet chapel set apart for silence and meditation even on feast days when the place bustled with visitors. There were times when the whole church was a waiting space empty of people and full of light and holiness; other times it filled up with footsteps and song, the leisurely river of chanting and the musical murmur of liturgical responses. Whatever the case, the small oratory remained folded away as a place of prayer, the heart hidden inside the ribs of this living place of worship, where a man might quietly and privately seek his God.

To the small oratory came the kitcheners or the infirmarians or the guest master, when their duties had obliged them to stay at their place of work and fail in their attendance in chapel for the office. Especially this was true for the infirmary brothers when anyone in their care was critically ill or an emergency arose; and of the kitchen brothers when, despite their best efforts to plan ahead, they had to skip Sext because it fell just before the midday meal or missed Vespers because it fell just before supper. Then they would come quietly into the small oratory and say the office alone as opportunity permitted.

The oratory was for anyone. People in the parish bearing burdens of grief or troubled mind would come and sit there in its hush, allowing the prayer that had seeped into the wood and the stones and hung upon the air to seep in its turn into their own souls, strengthening them. The small chapel was always open.

On that summer afternoon Madeleine found herself with no particular task urgently pressing, and she came with her rosary to the little oratory, to sit for a while and allow the gaze of Christ to search her heart. Father Theodore was her confessor now, and tomorrow she would go to him, as she had a month ago in mid-July, to seek his good counsel for her life. There is no point in having a confessor from whom one keeps secrets, and part of what had drawn Madeleine to the small oratory today was the difficult decision of how much it might be advisable to tell Theodore, and how much to keep to herself.

She had asked Father Theodore to be her confessor when she had been about three weeks at St. Alcuin's because she liked his face, and she saw that he was shy and gentle. She thought he would be an understanding man. She had met with him for the first time in mid-June, when her heart had been filled with mixed emotions: profoundly thankful for the security of her new home; still reeling from the horrors of the night after which she had fled her burnt cottage in Motherwell; and comforted and cheered by the new friendships she had found—especially with Father William, who was so good to her.

A month later when she saw Theodore in mid-July, the nightmare memories of Motherwell—and indeed almost everything else in life—had blurred into a vague backdrop roughed into the perimeter of her days. Her thoughts, her dreams, and her longing were filled incessantly by the bond that had grown between herself and William, overwhelming and unexpected. She felt like someone standing thigh deep in a place where the pounding breakers crash upon the shingle in the wild high seas of spring, struggling with only partial success to keep her footing, every moment increasing the likelihood of being swept away completely.

She knew she had come to live here as a blameless and godly spinster, to go unobtrusively about her calling of healing the sick, living under the shelter of her brother's integrity, eminence, and magnanimity, with humble gratitude. She understood very clearly what was expected of her, and nothing in her remained at all blind to the obvious unspoken condition that under no circumstances would it be thinkable that she should even give houseroom in her fantasies to the prospect of having an affair with one of the brothers of John's house.

Madeleine was grateful. She trusted in God, and she took seriously Christ's standards of honesty and good faith. She grasped the implications of her position, and she loved her brother. She had been glad to come to St. Alcuin's, glad of the chance to work among the villagers keeping mothers and babes safe when a child was born, easing the path out of this world for the dying, curing the ailments and crises of those who fell ill. She had not meant to fall in love, nor had she been discontented to live as she was. It felt lonely sometimes, but she had found companionship among her neighbors, especially old Mother Cottingham in the cottage next door—she had never in her life been restless or unhappy without a man of her own. The prejudice against her and her mother had forced upon her the vulnerability that threatens a woman with no wealth and no husband in any community. But though she had sought protection and security, it had never occurred to her to look for a husband, nor had she imagined that in her early forties she would have been successful if she had. Madeleine was not a natural celibate; she was not indifferent to the comfort and companionship of marriage, or its pleasures. It was just that her path had not traveled that way. Until now—when by some cruel twist of circumstance, she found herself wholly, completely, irrecoverably in love with a man she could not have.

In July when she had met with Father Theodore, she had thought it prudent to confide in him nothing of this. She had expressed her thankfulness at her new situation and told him that the memories that had tortured her had faded with remarkable speed—for which, thanks be to God. She had chosen not to say that what made her new home a heaven, made her days sweet and healed her soul of every wound, were the daily visits to her cottage of Father William. Madeleine knew well that all of us see what we want to see and reconstruct reality according to our own point of view. She knew that of no one is this more true than a man or a woman in love. She had accordingly hung onto enough common sense to accept that her feelings might not be reciprocated, and she knew that a feeling is not a sin. She was not obliged to confess it therefore, and she kept it to herself.

Now in mid-August as she prepared again to meet with her confessor, everything had changed. It was not about feelings anymore but about love expressed in a passion of kisses. Lodged in her heart was William's groan of longing as he held her close in his arms, his body melded to hers in the utter surrender of his love and the irresistible ardor of his desire. There was not a shadow of ambiguity in which to take refuge, no question at all concerning the nature of their relationship. There was no point in having a confessor if you kept something of this magnitude hidden from him. Presumably William was supposed to confess his state of soul to his abbot; Madeleine felt entirely certain that he would not be saying anything at all of this. So she did not know what to do, and she came to the small oratory to prepare for her confession and think through the implications both spiritual and practical of the possibilities open to her. One thing that she considered to be of crucial importance was that she absolutely trusted Father Theodore. She could read the faces and weigh the souls of her fellow human beings, and she knew in her bones that whatever she told him, he would not give her away. That meant her dilemma was not further complicated by uncertainty about her confessor's reliability. On the other hand, if she had not trusted him to keep silence, it would have made the decision easier; she would simply have kept silence herself.

Something else puzzled Madeleine, which was that Mother Cottingham had somehow changed. She had made Madeleine welcome from her first arrival, and a firm friendship had been forged between them. But recently something had been different. When the old woman looked at her, Madeleine detected something unspoken in her eyes. The friendship had not suffered from this; if anything, Madeleine saw a conspiratorial twinkle that had not been there before, and she could not help wondering if her ancient neighbor had somehow discerned what had passed between herself and William—but she did not see how this could be. Not by the least syllable or meaning look had Madeleine hinted at any kind of a special relationship, and she knew that neither William nor any other monk of St. Alcuin's would be seeking out an old woman to entrust with the secrets of his heart. And yet . . . Madeleine felt increasingly certain that Ellen knew something and wondered if, choosing her words carefully so as not to give anything away, she ought to ask her.

So she sat in the little oratory, turning over these things in her mind, praying the rosary and searching deeper, deeper . . . to find the right way forward, to keep her footing on a path of honesty in this treacherous and precarious country.

She had closed and latched the door when she came in. When anybody from the parish entered, the iron latch rattled loudly as they opened the door. Hearing but the faintest, barely audible click behind her, she knew it was one of the brothers who had entered. For a moment she felt guilty, lest she be unwelcome to a monk's need for prayer in the peace of solitude; but as she sensed the man hesitate on the step, then heard his feet make up their mind and come quietly along the aisle toward her, she knew exactly who it was. So she was not surprised when he came to stand just behind the bench where she sat, and she felt the feather-light caress of his hand on the back of her head.

Everything went on alert in Madeleine then. This, she knew, was courting peril beyond all good sense. Danger throbbed in every warning system of her soul and body. They must not be discovered. They must not. But at the same time, she yearned for his touch, to hear his voice, to spend even one snatched minute in his company.

He stepped over the low bench to sit beside her. She glanced at him, and her heart bucked and flipped when she saw the tenderness in his eyes and the defenseless self-offering of his love.

"William, this is unwise!" she whispered fiercely. "This is most unseemly!"

But she said nothing else because he took her in his arms and closed his mouth on hers in the slow, sweet rapture of his kiss. For that brief moment both of them stopped caring: he knew nothing but her; she knew nothing but him. Neither of them knew anything of Brother Cormac entering through the unlatched door and withdrawing as quietly as he had come in, on seeing his presence there to be inappropriate.

Not many minutes later, someone fumbled at the catch. By the time Brother Walafrid entered to spend a while in the quiet and say his rosary, there was nothing to see but Mistress Hazell sitting with head bent demurely in prayer and Father William doing his routine check of the altar silver. That done, William backed away, with a deep bow, from the altar and left with light, quiet step, without glancing at either Madeleine or Brother Walafrid.

William took his turn as a reader at the evening meal that day, and so he came into the kitchen afterward for the supper set aside for him by those who had prepared it.

Brother Conradus nodded to him pleasantly as they passed each other, Conradus with a heaped tray of bowls on his way to the scullery.

Brother Cormac stood by the table where meals had been set aside, and he picked up a bowl of food and a plate of bread and butter at William's approach. He stood holding these, and as William reached the table and he gave them into his hands, he did not release them immediately. Very direct, very level, his blue gaze met William's eyes. He said, in an undertone that nobody else could possibly have heard, "I had to miss the midday office and so came for my prayers into the little oratory after the meal, but I found I was intruding. You are skating on very thin ice, Brother. Our abbot is open and gentle, patient and kind, but he will not countenance this. Besides, he deserves better from you, and you are abusing the trust of all of us. I shall not rat on you, but I counsel you to think again."

William felt the familiar grip of terror in his belly and the slow flush of blood in his face.

He nodded. "Thank you," he said as Cormac released the bowl and the plate into his hands.

William retained enough sense of perspective to feel very grateful to Cormac for his manner of responding to what he had seen, and he hung on to that focus. But he also felt cornered, and wretched, and anxious. Since it was no longer in use for meal preparation, the readers and servers usually ate with the kitcheners at the big worktable in the kitchen, for a small group of men it felt more friendly than the spacious refectory. But William took his supper through to the frater, walking the length of the oak table to the most retired corner, where he could recover himself in solitude. He sat with the food before him on the table, but he could not eat a single mouthful. He faced the fact that the occasional stolen kiss was far, far too risky. There was no practical course to take other than absolutely renouncing this love in totality. He toyed with his bread, breaking it absently, but gazing beyond it at nothing, wondering hopelessly how to get out of this mess. He had no solutions and no expectation of finding any. He had nothing to offer Madeleine and nowhere to go. Nothing had changed since the last time his mind went round this treadmill. There was no way out. He was gradually realizing that what he had set himself to do was too much for him. He just could not renounce this love. It ached in him until he felt physically sick with longing, but whichever way he looked at it he was in no position to do anything other than give it up. He thought Madeleine deserved something better than the furtive deceit of stolen kisses; he was quite certain she deserved a better man than a monk breaking his vows while he exploited the goodwill of the community for his bed and board, took advantage of his abbot's belief in him, and tangled her in his net of lies with the direct intention of duping her brother who trusted her.

When he brought his mind back to the present moment, on a lesser level he also felt ashamed that he had taken the supper, then simply wasted the food. It was hard to get rid of it without the kitchen brothers, whose duty required them to stay in the kitchen until all had been cleaned and tidied away, seeing him dispose of it. He wished they'd go away. He wished it was possible to do anything at all without being observed by eyes that cared and would be bound to have an opinion. He wished his confessor was anybody but John. For a fleeting moment he wondered if it would have been better that he had never met Madeleine, but his heart cried, *No! No! No!* Somewhere deep in his gut he descended into frantic blind panic at the prospect of being torn apart from her. "Please," he whispered with bent head, his elbows on the table creating a tent of privacy as he put his hands to his temples, "Please don't take her away from me." He tried to set his lips firm and stare at nothing, to hold back the tears that usually waited until nightfall and the seclusion of his cell, and he felt like an animal in a trap. He knew that he could not face going back through the kitchen, and he could not stay here like this, and he could not eat this food. In the end, he swung his legs over the bench, got up leaving the plates of uneaten food behind for someone else to find and deal with, and left by the door that led out to the kitchen garden and the orchards, and from there to the path rising up to the farm and the burial ground. He walked swiftly, possessed by the need to be on his own, before the black flood of despair inside him swelled to the point where the dam must break.

Brother Conradus had worked extremely hard that day. He had made some excellent blackberry pies for supper, which had been well received—but he noticed to his disappointment that Father William had not even touched his bread and hearty bowlful of vegetable soup, nor even troubled to clear it away, which Conradus found irritating. And if he hadn't liked the soup, well he might still have fancied some blackberry pie. It took quite some effort for Brother Conradus to clear away the wasted food without comment when he went to wipe down the tables, and he had to say three Hail Marys before he could bring himself to add even an attempt at a charitable attitude to the already considerable self-discipline of refraining from passing any kind of remark to Brother Cormac. Brother Conradus knew from past experience that Brother Cormac's blistering turn of phrase could be very comforting when the best efforts of the kitchen went unappreciated, but only that morning Father Theodore had spoken to his novices about the forbearance that wants to go deeper than what we say or do, sinking right down inside to mature into an attitude of gentleness, a heart that understands and forgives. Conradus had thought that sounded so beautiful, and he could see that caustic observations about men who took good food and didn't eat it, and furthermore couldn't even be bothered to clear their own dishes, would not square with that beautiful spirit of forbearance. He threw the bread out for the birds, scraping the butter carefully back into the dish it had come from, tipping the soup into the pot with what already remained to be reused tomorrow.

He and Brother Cormac had washed up after the meal, and after they had left the kitchen all tidy, Brother Cormac had gone up to the guesthouse with some provisions needed there while Brother Conradus went to clear the scraps from the infirmary meal. Then it was time for Vespers—and afterwards, Conradus thought if he didn't manage to get some time out of doors he would just burst. He had spent the morning on his novitiate studies as usual and the afternoon reading *The Cloud of Unknowing* (incomprehensible) in his cell without once dozing off; he felt the day owed him an hour in the fresh air.

It was a beautiful evening, and he went into the kitchen garden to dig some weeds that were threatening to get out of hand. The low, slanting sun gave out a surprising amount of heat for the hour of the day, gladdening his spirit; he loved the sight of the small clouds drifting lazily across the still blue of the evening sky.

After a while he put down his gardening tools and washed his hands carefully in a bowl of water. He had brought the bowl out with him specially for this purpose, so that he wouldn't soil the well bucket, which should be kept completely clean. He had seen Brother Cormac in similar circumstances simply brush the surplus earth off by rubbing his hands on the skirts of his habit or giving them a quick wipe on his scapular, but though he held the professed brethren in the highest esteem, Brother Conradus knew for a fact that this was inadequate hygiene for a kitchener. He shook the shining drops of water from his hands and waved them about a bit to dry in the air, tossing the muddied water in the bowl onto one of the vegetable beds. Then he took off for a walk down the slope from the kitchen to the river. He could see it sparkling where the breeze rippled the surface and reflecting the colors slowly forming in the changing sky. He thought he had time to go for a stroll up the hill before Compline, and he walked along the riverbank from this broad stretch of water, up toward the narrower tumbling waters that splashed over the stones. Higher still and the river narrowed to a stream. The source of it was up on the moor, but Brother Conradus liked this particular part that ran through a belt of woodland circling round from behind the burial ground all the way to the edge of the farm. Ferns grew among the rocks, and birch and rowan trees sprang graceful from the peaty earth. As he climbed higher, the path took him into the trees. The birch leaves, little serrated arrowheads of summer green, flirted with the dappling light; the evening sunshine penetrated through the trees as an amber glow, finding a way into the depths of the wood with a sense of such timeless peace. He stopped walking and looked all around. He looked back the way he had come, down on the abbey nestling in the curve of the hills, its lichened roof and honey-colored stone lovely in the golden light. He looked down at the beck, jumping and gurgling, freshening the air. He looked into the wood that, though it was no more than a coppice really, still had enough depth for mystery.

Then Brother Conradus saw something. He looked twice because he thought his eyes had deceived him at first glance, but no—he was right. There in that cradled space where the ground rose and dipped, against the decaying trunk of a fallen tree, huddled in the leaves, resting his head against the moss that had colonized the dead wood, one of his brothers sat hunched. For some reason he could not exactly place, Brother Conradus formed the impression the man might be unwell, otherwise he would have assumed him to be praying quietly and respected his solitude.

As he drew nearer, concerned, he saw that the man, curled into a tight ball, had his face in his hands. And then it dawned on Conradus, who almost stood over him by now, that he was sobbing as if his heart would break. And he felt almost sure (though scrunched up like that with his back turned it was hard to say, several men had silver hair) it was Father William, the cellarer—well, the cellarer's assistant, but they all knew he was the cellarer really. Brother Conradus's heart flooded with pity, and he wanted to offer some comfort, but the longer he stood there, the less sure he felt that he ought to be there at all.

"Oh, Christ . . . my lord Christ . . . it is too much . . . too much . . . I cannot do it . . . ." Conradus heard the muffled groan before the convulsing sobs eradicated any kind of speech, and the conviction came to him that his presence here would be seriously unwelcome. He stepped backward cautiously, onto a large fallen twig that broke with a loud snap. The response this provoked made Conradus almost jump out of his skin.

William (it was he) flinched violently, and with an odd, sudden, sideways movement that reminded Brother Conradus of a frightened crab scuttling to safety in a rock pool, he reacted with alacrity, scrambling away from the sound and flinging himself round to face whoever had made it. This left him crouching like a cornered fugitive, aghast at being thus discovered.

As he looked down at William's face, red blotched and awash with tears, eyes swollen almost shut from weeping, but open enough to glitter at the novice in helpless rage at being thus run to ground, Brother Conradus could see immediately that he had messed this up to the maximum. Both startled, in a brief hiatus they regarded each other.

"Is there nowhere—nowhere at all in this monastery— where a man can ever find the shelter of a little privacy?" demanded William then. Those were not his exact words but the gist that remained once the multiple expletives that peppered his question had been overlooked.

Brother Conradus, appalled to find he had so seriously blundered with his unwelcome intrusion, stammered his apology and began to back away. William's furious, desperate, tragic face looked like a wild creature at bay—quite a savage one.

With great courage, Conradus paused in his retreat. "Father, you seem to be in such trouble," he ventured bravely. "Is there nothing I can do to help?"

"'No!" William snarled at him, "except go away and leave me in peace and keep this to yourself!"

Conradus nodded. "*Mea culpa*," he said humbly, and smote his breast. "Please forgive me for having intruded."

He retreated with all haste and hurried back down the hill, his joy in the evening eclipsed by the disconcerting experience. The memory of it stayed with him through Compline and followed him into the Great Silence of the night. He was glad when, after Chapter the next morning, the silence lifted and the comfortable banter of his companions in the novitiate reestablished his sense of normality. He did not divulge anything of what he had seen but put it as best as he could from his mind. He did not especially like William and felt afraid of him if anything, but he had no wish to expose anyone's private grief to community gossip.

After the midday meal the next day, he felt drowsy. The air was muggy and humid; distant thunder rumbled up on the hills. Nothing moved, and the heat felt oppressive. He was permitted a siesta in the afternoons provided he attended to his own studies as well as his work in the kitchen. So he snatched a short nap in his cell, which extended longer than he had meant, and then dashed down to help Brother Cormac prepare the evening meal. At least that was what he told himself. Brother Conradus regarded all the fully professed brothers with proper respect and did not admit even to himself that his haste in reaching the kitchen was as much to prevent Cormac from having too great a hand in the meal preparation as to help him. But he found all well. Baked fish and salad greens were not complex dishes and asked for no sophisticated level of expertise. The dishes went covered into the embers of the fire, and Brother Cormac said he'd get the bowls of fruit ready if Conradus would dish up the bread for the servers to take into the refectory.

Brother Conradus had put out thirty-eight portions of bread and was in process of deftly and methodically adding to each plate an appropriate helping of butter when he became aware of someone's presence on the other side of the large table that held all the plates. Assuming it would be Brother Cormac, he glanced up and was taken aback to find himself looking into William's eyes. He knew it was ridiculous that this man's gaze always gave him a slight sense of alarm: but, exacerbated as this was by the unsettling encounter of the evening before, he stopped breathing completely, his hand holding the knife with its load of butter arrested in midair.

William's eyes appeared to search his soul. Conradus thought he looked very slightly unhinged. He observed that William had broken a blood vessel in his left eye; the effect was decidedly macabre. Taken all round, he looked dreadful.

"I am so very, very sorry," said William. "I should never have spoken to you as I did. Please will you forgive me?" He spoke with such humility and contrition that Conradus was even further astounded.

The young man blinked, recollected himself sufficiently to close his mouth, swallowed, and said, "Think nothing of it. I'm sorry to have put my foot in it as I did."

He knew that monastic apologies and absolutions were not supposed to go like this. There was a form, a ritual, and every brother should stick to it, but he could see this would not be the moment to insist upon it.

William nodded. A brave gleam of something suggestive of a smile warmed his features, but not very much. He half turned to go, then hesitated and turned back. "Please—you won't . . . "

"No," Conradus reassured him. "No, I won't."

But though he would not have dreamed of telling of what he had seen, as a juicy tidbit of gossip, the more he thought about it, the more convinced he became that he ought to make sure their abbot knew all was not well with Father William's soul. He did not act on this instinct immediately. He knew well enough how a secret burns and tries the doors to be let out. He kept it to himself for another ten days, doing every little thing he could think of in the meanwhile to bring comfort to Father William—but with notable lack of success. Then when Father Theodore took the novices through the chapters of the Rule laying down the monastic duty of confiding all things to the abbot in absolute trust and without reserve, Brother Conradus knew where his duty lay.

As Conradus stood the closest he could get to the other side of John's table, gazing at him urgently, Abbot John reflected that this young man's dark eyes were very compelling.

He leaned back in his chair, putting down his pen, to listen to what the novice had to say.

"It's Father William," said Brother Conradus.

"Oh? What now?" John waited with a certain amount of apprehension for what fresh revelation there might be.

"I believe . . . " Conradus fixed his abbot with the trusting, ardent fervency of his eyes, " . . . that he is very unhappy!"

On the receiving end of the unconscious melodrama in the short, plump young man's voice, in the earnest solicitude in his eyes, in his sense of complete involvement with the distress he had detected, John was appalled to find that he wanted to laugh. It was not that William's struggle didn't matter to him; he was acutely aware of it, and not a day passed without him praying for William and usually reappraising his own pastoral management of the situation, asking himself if he had done as he should and all he could. What activated his sense of the ridiculous was the young man's fervid engrossment that struck John as more than a little sensationalist and out of proportion. It had not escaped his attention that William had lost the joy that had briefly illumined him, but John, having little to do with him in these last few weeks, had seen him only return to his habitual appearance of dry, ironic detachment. Manfully holding down the rising wave of mirth that having been triggered threatened to get out of hand, he defused the vibrancy of energy by reaching for the rag to clean his pen and moving it to a different place on the table.

"Yes," he replied, unable to look at Conradus, "he does have a rather doleful cast of countenance at times, doesn't he?" With considerable effort, John kept his face straight, but his voice shook.

"No!" John felt the combined force of Brother Conradus's depth of compassion and powerful sense of duty converging upon him. "I mean, *really* unhappy. The sort of unhappiness even food cannot touch. Father, in this last month I have tried every means to comfort and cheer him. I have taken him little pastries and delicious date truffles, I have made him lovely spiced cordials and tasty morsels—flowers fried in batter, tiny plum turnovers, everything I could think of. I even—" John kept his eyes fixed determinedly on the edge of his table, but he could feel the novice leaning over it toward him. "—in final desperation I made the secret recipe that the Lady Giacoma di Settesoli made for the blessed Francis of Assisi at his own request in the last extremis of his dying! I mean, he received the holy sacrament, of course!" Shocked at himself, Conradus hastened to correct any unintentional impression he might have conveyed that Francesco Bernadone could be considered by any person to be naturally frivolous. "But before that, his soul was upheld and comforted by the confection—and who could have been less fixated upon his victuals than the blessed Francis? I thought it couldn't fail: but it did! Father William took one look at it and asked me to take it away. But he didn't ask me gently, or decline it with courtesy. His tone was rough and the words he used unrepeatable—and he doesn't normally speak with a harsh voice; his speech is characteristically soft and light. I concluded, he is struggling with something terrible, some dark oppression or distress. And I have *seen* that he is. I cannot tell you because I said I wouldn't, but I have seen that he *is really unhappy*."

This proved too much for John. The spectacle of this serious novice with his indefatigable solicitude for William's well-being, presenting himself with an unending parade of unwelcome delicacies at every end and turn, came so vividly before the abbot's imagination that he collapsed in helpless laughter.

"Oh, I'm so sorry, Brother Conradus," he gasped when he could speak, "I do beg your pardon! Oh, glory—just a minute . . . " But he could still see the situation in his mind's eye, and the inherent comedy of it just made him laugh the more.

He could feel the young novice's hurt bewilderment and, when he eventually got enough of a grip on himself to look up at him, saw that he was really offended.

"Forgive me—please forgive me," he said. "I'm not belittling what you've told me, it's just that I can so vividly see . . . " He shook his head as the laughter rose inside him again.

"I know he's unhappy," he managed to say eventually. "He does talk to me. He has troubles of his own that go deep into his heart. Flowers fried in batter won't really suffice . . . . Besides, I think he's really more of a red wine and strong cheese and roast pigeon man—but you'd do best not to take him anything. I'm sure he will be touched by your kindness, but when he's hurting he usually wants to be left alone."

Brother Conradus took in these words. He supposed there might be a funny side to his efforts to console Father William, though he couldn't really see it himself. And he had heard that there are people in this life for whom food is nothing more than sustenance, not the comfort and delight it was for Brother Conradus, who regarded mealtimes as the highlights of the day. He realized he must have met one such person in Father William.

"What can I do for him then?" he asked sadly.

John smiled at him. "You do my heart good, Brother—you are so kind. I'll wager your kindness *has* been a comfort to Father William even if he spurned the tidbits you brought him. He's a complicated man. I think you should pray for him and leave him in peace."

Brother Conradus nodded soberly. "I haven't—have I—Father, do you think I might have made things worse? I didn't mean to—"

"He is not so churlish that he cannot appreciate gentleness," his abbot reassured him. "You have not made anything worse; he's just touchy and oversensitive. Don't let it prey on your mind. He'll find a way through his difficulties in the end. And thank you for having the concern for him to come and ask me about it."

"It says in the Rule . . . " Some of the eagerness returned to Conradus's eyes. " . . . it says that we are to confide in you and bring you our burdens."

"Well, yes," said John, "and that's an immense privilege and very daunting at the same time. I don't think I've quite grown into being an abbot yet; I still feel like just me."

Conradus smiled at him. "'Only John, who loves to heal people.' That's what you said to me before, and that's how I pray for you."

"Thank you. Thank you so much, Brother. And thank you for your kindness to Father William—kindness goes a long way in a monastery; we rest gratefully on each other's kindness in the tough times. Only, it has to be expressed with restraint. So long as you go on being patient with him, understanding of his incivility when he's feeling morose, that's the main thing. And pray for him."

"I do pray for him," said Brother Conradus. "I pray every day. But I didn't know what to pray for because I don't know what's wrong. So I asked Our Lady—Our Lady of Sorrows— what he needed. And it came into my mind that I should pray that he would have the courage to keep the flower of his love alive through this winter, for it would have its time in the sun. Those were the words that came to me, and even though it seemed odd—because it isn't winter, is it?—that's what I pray for every day."

The expression on his abbot's face changed, and Conradus saw that he had touched upon something important. For a moment John said nothing, taking in what the novice had said to him.

"You—you truly know nothing of Father William's private concerns?" he asked sharply.

"Nothing at all, Father. That's why I asked Our Lady."

Conradus could see that John felt very disconcerted by this, but his abbot deemed it prudent to close off the conversation.

"Well, thank you for praying for him. It always makes a difference. Every time. And thank you for coming to see me and for trusting me with your concerns. I'm sorry I laughed—it just struck me funny; it's not that I don't care. I'll make a time to see him. Was there anything else?"

Brother Conradus hesitated.

"Well?"

"It's something else about Father William. There is something more."

John waited. He thought they had probably discussed Father William quite enough and wished he hadn't asked.

"He feels afraid." Brother Conradus spoke softly, and this time he would not look at John. "And sometimes he feels that he is worth nothing. And I think somewhere people have held him in contempt, for he is full of shame."

He risked a glance at John. "I just wanted you to know."

John had not entertained precise expectations of his conversations as their abbot with the young men in the novitiate, but he certainly hadn't imagined something like this.

"What makes you say so?" he inquired cautiously. "Father William hasn't been discussing this with you, has he?" Nothing in John could envisage a scenario in which William might confide in a novice, but he thought he'd better ask.

"No," said Brother Conradus. "Never. But often when he has to speak to me on any matter, I have noticed that he makes me feel ashamed, and frightened, and worthless somehow, as though he held me in contempt. And then when he goes away, so does the feeling. But I know he doesn't mean to. And my mother . . . my mother used to say that you can tell what people feel inside by how they make you feel when you are with them. She said that a person has nothing to give you but what is within their heart, so if they are afraid, they have nothing to give you but fear, and they put it into your heart too. That's what she said."

His abbot considered this. "Have I—I haven't met your mother, have I, Brother Conradus?"

The novice shook his head. "No, Father. She has many responsibilities at home, and we are not wealthy. It would be difficult for her to make the journey here, for we live twenty miles away. I came here by myself. And anyway, that was when Father Chad was standing in while we waited for you. No, you haven't met my mother."

"I hope I do one day," said Father John, "for I think I would like her very much. Is that all then?"

And this time Brother Conradus said yes, he had nothing else on his mind.

As he walked along the cloister away from the abbot's lodge, Conradus felt he had been right to have laid his concern for Father William before his abbot, but it saddened him to think there was no comfort he could offer. He resolved to hold before his mind the words that had arisen within him and enfold Father William in prayer on every possible occasion until whatever it was that so oppressed his soul had been driven away.

After the young man had gone, John sat in thought without moving for some while. Afraid. Unhappy. Worthless. Full of shame. He wondered how much of it was Brother Conradus's imagination. Even so, somehow . . . it didn't sound good. At the very least it seemed that William had been less than gentle with this novice on several occasions. In a sudden, swift movement of decision, he left the unfinished work on his table and went out through the door to the abbey court, heading for the checker. He got halfway there, then his footsteps slowed. Almost there, he stopped, changed his mind, and turned back along the way he had come. He wanted to speak to Brother Cormac first, though he was not sure of finding him in the kitchen at this time of the day. It seemed prudent to reassure himself, before opening the matter with William, that Brother Conradus's motives could entirely be trusted.

The long wall of the refectory had a door onto the abbey court, so John went in there as the quickest route to the kitchen and came upon Brother Cormac and Father William going through the weekly check of the knives and spoons.

"Well met! I was looking for both of you!"

They looked up and stopped the count, but John said, "No, no! I won't interrupt you—well, no more than I already have. I need to speak with you, Brother Cormac, and I'll just wait here for that until you've finished; it's only something quick. Father William, if you are free to do so, will you call into my house after None? Thank you. There's something I needed to talk over with you. I'll sit and wait here until you're done—no rush."

Having satisfied himself that nothing had been lost, broken, or stolen, William thanked Brother Cormac, inclined his head in a movement of flawless courtesy to John, and was on his way as Cormac returned the utensils to the kitchen. Watching William as he interacted with Brother Cormac, John tried to evaluate what he observed as dispassionately as he could. He could see that a novice might find him intimidating; his entire demeanor was of a man who took no prisoners. His tone was brisk and neutral, not especially friendly. There was nothing in him to reassure or encourage, except when he deliberately put it there, which most of the time he did not. But that didn't appear to bother Cormac; they seemed easy together.

"So. How can I help you?" Cormac was back from the kitchen and wiping his hands on his apron. Looking at him John was not sure which would come off worse, the apron or the hands, but he thought that might be a matter for another day.

"Would you close the door, Brother?" asked John. "It doesn't matter if we are interrupted, but I would rather not be unknowingly overheard."

Cormac went back and closed the door and came to sit on the bench on the other side of the table from John, braced for a scolding. He had no idea what he might have done wrong, but he couldn't think of any other reason his abbot might want to speak with him in private.

"Tell me what you think of Father William."

Brother Cormac looked at him, startled. He hadn't been expecting that.

"Um . . . in general? Or with regard to anything in particular?"

The caution in Cormac's voice alerted John. He felt glad he'd asked.

"In general. Though if there's anything in particular you've seen, you might tell me."

John was surprised by Cormac's reaction to this. He had imagined this interview would be easy and short. He would say, *What do you think of Father William?* And Brother Cormac would say, *Efficient but fairly hard work* or some such thing, because this was simply the preamble to what he really wanted to ask him. But the unexpected reticence in Cormac's eyes told him he'd stumbled on more that he'd been looking for.

"He . . . Father William fulfills his work meticulously." Brother Cormac was finding his way with a puzzling degree of caution. "He can be . . . well, he is . . . Father William can be brusque on occasion."

John looked hard at his kitchener, who met his eyes with his own level gaze that gave nothing away.

"Is something the matter? Have you had some kind of altercation with Father William?" John probed further and was even more puzzled to see a look of relief enter Brother Cormac's eyes.

"No," he said with conviction. "Never. No, I haven't."

"And there is nothing else you want to tell me about him?"

"No, Father, there is not."

What? thought John. *What is it?* He was not set at ease by the look of helpful innocence that Cormac's face now wore. But whatever it was his kitchener felt was better left unsaid, John thought he stood very little chance of prying it out of him. Brother Cormac was not that kind of man.

"Is he courteous with the men in the kitchen? Is he helpful? Is he pleasant?"

Cormac's face lit up in a grin of pure merriment at that. "Father William? Those would not have been the first words I'd have picked to describe him, if I'm honest. But he's not exactly discourteous or unhelpful or unpleasant—he just does his job. He comes in here and we're glad when he's gone, but there's no harm in him."

John nodded. "I understand. And tell me now—how would you describe Brother Conradus?"

Again Cormac smiled. "A godsend, I should think. He is . . . now let me think. I was going to say the word that comes to my mind when I think of Brother Conradus is 'enthusiasm,' but that's not quite right. He certainly has more enthusiasm for almost anything than anyone else I know, but the word that sums him up best is 'kind.' Brother Conradus is a soul of pure kindness. It's a pleasure to work with him, and I hope he decides to make full profession here and stay with us always."

"And can I ask you—there is no guile in Brother Conradus? He would never in your view try to manipulate anyone?"

This made Brother Cormac laugh. "No," he said. "He would not."

"Thank you." His abbot looked satisfied with this. "That's all I wanted to know. And you yourself? All is well with you?"

Brother Cormac assured him that it was, and they rose each to go about his own business, Cormac in the kitchen garden where he wanted to take the pea haulm down to be threshed, and John to the checker—his conversation with Cormac about

Conradus had been shorter than he thought it could have been, and he did not want to return to other matters until he had sorted this thing out.

He found William in the checker haggling with a cord-wainer over a better price for winter boots. John nodded good day to Brother Ambrose and gestured to him to remain seated and carry on as normal, then moved a miscellany of items from a stool to a small unoccupied space on the counter running the length of the room along the wall opposite the door. He sat on the stool and waited quietly, watching William. The tradesman didn't stand a chance. He went away looking crestfallen, with a good order that he had clearly needed, but at a price that would leave him working long hours for very little profit at all. William bade him a formal, brief, courteous farewell, then turned to his abbot.

"I'm so sorry, Father John," he said. "I had not meant to keep you waiting."

"You haven't," replied John, thinking how different was William's demeanor from the days that seemed so long ago now, when they traveled to Motherwell and brought Madeleine home, and Oswald. The glimpse into the warm and vivid personality he had caught was lost; William had retreated behind locked shutters, it seemed.

"I just came to see if you could spare the time to see me now. I was finished earlier than I thought."

William readily assented and, without bothering with any parting pleasantry to Brother Ambrose, left the checker with his abbot.

"I thought you pushed that cobbler a bit hard," John remarked.

"Yes," said William, "that's my job. I'm here to make our finances work, to earn us money and save us money and keep our coffers protected and full."

John did not reply immediately. Then he ventured, "You do

that well, and I am—we all are—grateful. But there are other currencies than money. If you take care to accrue goodwill, it is a standby when money fails, and it sweetens life and oils the wheels of trade relationships even when there is money in the bank."

William had no answer for this. It had not occurred to him to think along these lines.

They reached the abbot's lodge in silence. William leaned forward to open the door, then stood aside respectfully to allow his superior to precede him. John felt uneasy. He thought Cormac was right. There was nothing to complain of: William was punctiliously polite. But his manner had no warmth; it was closed and guarded.

"Sit you down," said John, and indicated the chairs by the hearth. The two men sat down together.

William looked at him, waiting. John tried to think of some general conversation to ease the way into what he wanted to say and could not. So, "Brother Conradus has been to see me," he said, and William looked immediately wary.

There's something, thought John, something with these kitchen brothers . . . something these men are choosing not to tell me.

"He is concerned for you."

"Oh?" William's face and tone remained studiedly neutral.

"Yes. He says that he believes you to be extremely unhappy. He preferred not to enlarge further on why. I am assuming that the cause of your unhappiness is what I think it is. Would there be anything else?"

"There is nothing else," said William. His words sounded very final.

John nodded. "Then I am sorry you are unhappy, but there is nothing, I think, that you or I can do. In due course, time will heal that sadness. To renounce a love is not an easy thing."

"No," said William.

John nodded again. He persisted, "Brother Conradus also told me that he believes you feel . . . let me see . . . 'afraid,' he said, and 'full of shame' and 'not worth very much.' And he said he thought there had been times when you had been treated with contempt."

He looked for, and saw, the telltale flicker of William's eyes that let him know those observations were accurate and had surely found their mark. "Speak to me about that, William," he prompted softly.

"Why does he say so?" asked William. "I mean, yes, he's right. I am often afraid, I have plenty to be ashamed of, and I should judge that contempt has regularly featured in the opinion others hold of me. You know all those things. What's new?"

He paused. "I ask your pardon, Father. I didn't mean to sound so rude."

"He says so," said John carefully, gently, "because his mother, he tells me, taught him that you can tell how another person feels from how they make you feel."

William leaned forward in the chair, his arms resting on his knees, his hands clasped together. The shift in position served to hide his face from John, but not before John saw the shadow of weariness and pain.

"Brother Conradus," John continued, "has not complained of you. I realize well enough how common it is for a man to inform on his brother covertly under guise of expressing concern, but Brother Conradus is not that kind of man. His concern for you is real. Only, I cannot help seeing, and I'm sure you must see too, that you must have been more than a little surly and curt with Brother Conradus, on more than a few occasions, to cause him to register in himself a sense of shame and fear and a feeling of being held in contempt. Would that be fair?"

William swallowed. "Yes," he said quietly. "I've no doubt it would."

I love your courage, thought John, and I love your honesty.

"Then I think," he said, gently still, "that you owe him an apology. Meanwhile—is there any way in this that I can be of help? Do you want to tell me anything? Is there anything I don't know?"

William sat up straight and looked at him.

"Oh, there's plenty you don't know," he said, "but nothing I want to tell you."

And John surmised from this, as William intended he should, that the summer had been a struggle, and it hurt badly to turn away from Madeleine.

"Well, my brother," said John softly, "I think you must go and say you're sorry. He's only a lad. He knows nothing of your grief. It isn't fair for him to feel the sharp end of your sorrow."

William inclined his head in assent. "Can it wait until I've finished what I was doing? I'll go today, but not right now, if that's all right. I—if it makes things any better—for what it's worth—I'm not altogether insensible. I know I can be . . . well . . . this won't be the first time I've apologized to him."

"Any time today," Abbot John gave his permission.

✠   ✠   ✠

Brother Cormac deftly chopped the herbs and green leaves for the salad. A handful of seeds and one of pine nuts went in, and he covered the bowls, fetched the oil, the vinegar, and the salt, and set them nearby to be added just before the food went to the tables.

"Where is Brother Conradus?"

Cormac glanced up briefly. He had not heard William's approach. "In the garden, watering the beans," he replied, reaching for a towel to dry his hands. He looked again at William. *Faith! Man in a foul mood*, he thought, and wished he'd been a bit vaguer about Conradus's whereabouts.

"Is there a problem?" he asked.

"No," said William, and he left by the door to the yard.

He walked across the cobbles softened with casual wildflowers at this time of year. Small plants grew round the base of the well. He went through the gap in the hedge into the kitchen garden and saw there Brother Conradus, patiently ministering to the vigorous plants as they bloomed on their tall sticks, with his buckets and pitchers of well water. Turning from the vegetable bed to the path, the novice caught sight of William making his way toward him, and his appearance altered from cheerful contentment to frozen apprehension. He found all the professed brothers inherently awe inspiring to the level of alarm: this one was worse than that. He felt suddenly frightened in case Abbot John had said something that might have made Father William angry with him. He stood on the path awaiting his doom as William walked down toward him.

William stopped in front of him and looked at the ground for a moment. His expression Conradus read as exasperated and irritable. Conradus wondered which thing he might have done had offended him this time.

William was in fact searching without success for some friendly pleasantry to set the novice at his ease. But his mind was empty. He was simply enduring this.

So without any niceties in advance, he knelt on the path before the young man.

"I have spoken to you ungratefully and unkindly," he said. "'Surly' was the word Father Abbot used, and that was accurate. I humbly beg your pardon, my brother. Please forgive me. Again. Please forgive me for doing no better than before. You are teaching me that my habits are selfish and ungracious. Thank you for that, but I beg your pardon. Of your charity, forgive me."

"*God*," thought Conradus. *He didn't say "God." You're supposed to say, "I ask God's forgiveness and yours, my brother."*

So, do I say God forgives him too, or is it just me that's meant to forgive him? Why doesn't he ever do this according to the rules?

William remained kneeling before him, his head bent. Looking down on the nape of his neck, Conradus was seized by an unexpectedly overwhelming wave of compassion. The nape of a man's neck looks so vulnerable, so defenseless. He had an idea that William didn't give a stuff about the tradition and probably thought his relationship with God was something to be fixed privately, but his contrition was not just a hollow shell of words; Conradus could see that. In the course of his childhood he had often enough witnessed how one of his brothers or sisters, forced by their mother to offer an apology, could fill the gentle words with contempt or even use them to convey a threat. This, he recognized, was something different. William meant what he said.

Before he could think what reply to frame, seeing that William had not asked the right question, Conradus was further startled by his looking up into his eyes. Brother Conradus himself never raised his face to look at the brother whose forgiveness he was required to seek. The experience felt penetrating enough already; it didn't need intensifying. And he had never seen anybody else do it either. Father Theodore hadn't said, but Conradus thought you were probably supposed to keep your head bent, for humility. He was beginning to feel out of his depth with this brother.

"Please," William said, and there was such a world of weariness and sadness in his face.

Brother Conradus thought since this professed brother had made up something and not used the proper form of words, then it might come across as more sincere and less of a formality if he did the same. So, "It's all right," he said. "God forgave you every time as soon as you said it, and I forgave you on average about three hours later. Be at peace; it's done with. It was my fault really. I hadn't grasped that you don't like sweetmeats. I won't pester you again."

And that seemed to be enough. William got to his feet. "Thank you," he said, and again Conradus thought he sounded as though he meant it, and yet his voice was dull, as though he could hardly bring himself to think anything.

"Brother," said Conradus in a rush of bravery, knowing he should have said "Father" and that it was probably something William would regard as none of his business anyway, and deciding not to care, "*Whatever* is it? You look as if something's completely crushing you."

"Crushing?" Something that Conradus assumed was intended as a smile crossed William's face. "You mean I don't look completely crushed yet? Well, that's an encouragement. Thank you for your charity, brother, and your patience. Maybe I should make a time to see you once a week before Mass and get all my apologies out of the way in one go. Thank you. You have a gentle spirit."

And with a sketchy suggestion of a respectful bow, he turned on his heel and went back up the path the way he had come.

"I'm sorry, brother," said Cormac who was waiting for Brother Conradus when he returned the pitchers to the scullery. "I didn't think quick enough to avoid that one."

"No—it was all right," the novice responded. "He wasn't angry. He wanted to say sorry for being rude to me again. But he seems so—do *you* know what's the matter with him, Brother Cormac?"

"Probably," said Cormac, "if I think about it. But it might be better not to, so I don't."

He reached past Brother Conradus for a large cooking pot hanging on a nail in the wall. "I'll boil some eggs," he said firmly, and Conradus realized he would have to be content with that enigmatically unsatisfying reply.

CHAPTER THREE

September

Madeleine stepped through the open door into the checker this mellow September morning, the scent of autumn carried on the light breeze, the earth lazy in the golden warmth of the day.

"God give you good day, Brother Ambrose!" she greeted him pleasantly. "How goes the work? Are we solvent? Are we walking in hope? Are we in profit?"

He looked up and smiled at her. "Good morrow, Mistress Hazell! I think I can say we are striding confidently—all our debts are paid, and we have enough in store for the unexpected; all repairs are done and accounts up to date. It's a marvel—but 'tisn't I. We have to thank Father William; the work he's put in takes my breath away. I never thought I'd see the day when we had everything in such exemplary order."

"Oh," said Madeleine, "he's got more to him than a pretty face and a charming manner then?"

Brother Ambrose chuckled, mightily amused by the suggestion that William could be considered as having either. "What can I do for you, Mistress Hazell, this fine day?"

"Well, with your permission, Brother Ambrose, it's not your time I came to waste but Father William's. Only for a moment. I've a message for him from Mother Cottingham."

"Surely—there he is in his corner, hard at work as we like him to be."

With a smile of thanks, Madeleine turned to William. She knew exactly where he was. She knew where he sat—and how he sat, and the look on his face when he was thinking or puzzling over some complication in his correspondence. She could feel him in all her body, even before she turned to look at him. She knew what he would be doing—calmly continuing apparently to address himself to the matters he had in hand until the moment she turned. And as she did so, he would raise his face to her with a carefully composed expression of polite inquiry that did not quite match the intensity in his eyes. And this he did.

"Madeleine," he said, "I am all yours."

She saw the amusement on his face at her sudden look of alarm before she registered that Brother Ambrose would take this for the harmless pleasantry it was not. She felt annoyed with herself (and with him) that the unexpected words left her slightly flustered—actually physically took her breath away—and that he saw. She felt very grateful in that moment to have her back to Brother Ambrose, the expression on her face obscured from his view.

"God give you good day, Father William," she said—and could think of no double entendre to match his, though for a few seconds she did frantically try. "Two things. The first is, yesterday I was in the infirmary taking them some good physic herbs from my garden, and Brother Michael said could I slip into the conversation in passing if I saw you that Father Oswald feels a little hurt (Brother Michael thinks) that you have not been to spend time with him in a while. Though why Brother Michael expects I am more like to run into you than he is, I cannot imagine."

William nodded. He read the warning in her words and in her eyes, telling him that the bond between them had not gone unnoticed among the brothers. "Thank you. I understand. Yes,

I'll go to see Oswald. He seems to be doing well; I have been somewhat preoccupied—had things on my mind—and thought I would not be much company for him. The other thing? Mother Cottingham?"

"She said—I am telling you exactly what she said—that she wanted to talk to you about sin."

"Really? Well, that's always a pleasure. I'll go over and see her this afternoon."

"She hasn't been too well this last week. She has a head cold, and it's gone to her chest a bit. But she wraps up warm and sits out in the afternoon sunshine when the wind doesn't blow, and I am taking good care of her. I'm going to beg some broth from Brother Cormac to make her a chicken soup—none of my hens have been broody yet; I've bred no pot fowls."

William leaned back in his chair as she talked, his face hidden from Brother Ambrose's line of vision by Madeleine standing there, his eyes frankly adoring her. Her words trailed away, disconcerted from her attempts to sound normal by the ardor that enfolded her like an embrace even as she stood in the middle of the room. She felt cherished, she felt wooed, she felt as though she'd been kissed.

"Well, that's all," she said.

"As soon as ever I can, if I can find a way to get free of all this," he replied softly, the yearning of his heart in his voice.

"Good Lord, brother, go easy on yourself!" Brother Ambrose laughed. "You work too hard! We can spare you for an hour to see poor old Mother Cottingham—think of it as an investment; the dear soul is good enough to us!"

"Ah—thanks, Ambrose; yes, that's the way to look at it. I'll be over to see her later today. Madeleine, thank you so much for stopping by."

Nothing in his words emphasized that last sentence, only the look in his eyes.

"She will wait for you until you can come to her, whenever

that may be," Madeleine said, her eyes and her tone having the same incongruence as his, and inclining her head in courteous farewell, she turned away.

"Don't work too hard, Brother Ambrose!" she said airily. "Why keep a dog and bark yourself?" And that gave her a reason for one last glance back at William, to take and store the smile she brought to his face in her heart.

William watched her leave, his eyes following her until she had gone through the door and turned the corner out of his sight.

"A pleasant woman," Brother Ambrose remarked. William looked at him, considering his words, his face betraying nothing.

"Yes," he said, "and it's a blessing to our kitchen to have the occasional pail of surplus milk from her goat."

He reached across the table for the wax and seal, to close the letters their abbot had already approved and signed and stamped.

When they rose from their work for the midday office and meal, Brother Ambrose commented on the beauty of the day; it seemed to make things go more cheerily, he thought—there had been a good atmosphere that morning in the checker.

When they had eaten, William made his way across to the abbey close, where he found Mother Cottingham's door ajar. He knocked, and a wheezy voice from within bade him enter.

He was aware of a sense of relief deep in his inner core as he stepped through her door. Here was someone who knew his longing and his sorrow and did not regard it as something to be suppressed or put away—not a cause of scandal but a valid love. He felt himself relaxing as he came in to see her. But it was not like Ellen Cottingham to let a visitor walk in without coming to greet him, and when he saw her, he stopped dead where he was.

"God love you, Mother—you look really unwell! I hadn't

realized. I'm so sorry; I should have come before." William's sense of shock was evident in his face. Her face was flushed and puffy and her eyes fever bright. The labor of her breathing was audible from just within the doorway. Three swift steps took him across the small room to her side, and he bent over her and kissed her brow tenderly, as if he had been her son. This meant the world to Ellen.

"Nay, I'm well enough. Your Madeleine has cared for me night and day. I'm that stuffed with herbs I feel like a fowl ready to go in the oven. I'm better than I was yesterday, and tomorrow I shall be still better again. Anyway, I'm always better for seeing thee."

He smiled at her, and she saw his real affection and felt it an honor.

"Madeleine tells me you want to talk to me about sin! What have you been up to?"

She looked at him. He found it impossible to read what she was thinking, so he sat down across the table from her and waited to hear whatever she wanted to tell him.

"That's why I didn't go out to sit in the sunshine this afternoon. I wanted to speak to thee in private. 'Tisn't my sin that's on my mind; I was thinking of thee."

"Lord have mercy on us—is it a sin to even *think* of me now? I must be getting worse."

She laughed, which made her wheezing worse and started her coughing. She sat for a while getting her breath back and took a sip of water from the small pewter mug that stood on the table at her side.

"That's enough, young man. I haven't much strength even though I'm on the mend. Listen to me now. It came to me in the night—not last night, the night before when I was really poorly—that I must talk to thee. What was thy mother like?"

William's eyebrows rose. "My mother? What has she to

do with anything? In Christian charity I think I should not describe my mother to anyone. And I don't know if it's 'was' or 'is.' I last spoke to her about thirty years ago."

"So you were not close—she and thee? You did not talk—as thou and I are talking now?"

William laughed—-not an especially pleasant laugh. "No," he said.

"And tha hast no sisters? Tha's not grown up with women?"

William shook his head. "Women have been distant stars to me, Mother. They shine all the brighter for that."

Ellen smiled but would not let herself laugh. The coughing hurt her chest. "Thee—tha'rt all rogue! Charming and wicked; I know thy kind!"

"It's true, I confess—but in spite of it the company of women has passed me by."

Ellen regarded him speculatively. "Well, then, art tha ready to hear what I have to say?"

"For sure. I'm listening."

"One more question first. Before tha came into a house of religion—or since—did tha lie with women? Has tha had lovers before?"

"Before what? Madeleine—or you?"

She chuckled, the net of wrinkles around her eyes closing in laughter, but she said, "Nay, lad, tha must take me seriously. This is important, and tha'rt hedging. Did tha?"

William felt the flush of color rise in his face, and he so wished this wouldn't happen—he hated the way it betrayed his loss of equilibrium.

"No," he said.

"Tha'rt a virgin then?"

"Mother Ellen—wherever is this leading? Yes, I—I suppose I'm a virgin. By a bishop's precise definition. I must confess I associate virginity with purity—a clean mind and heart, and I make no claim to that; but no, since you ask, I have never lain with a woman."

She nodded. "Then that's what I want to talk to thee about. It may be tha will be a monk all thy life. But from what tha's told me, I understand that if the chance ever comes thy way, tha'll make thy life with Madeleine. Am I right?"

William could not remember a time since he had left boyhood behind when anyone's questioning had made him feel so thoroughly uncomfortable and exposed. He could only answer her in the affirmative, but she saw his sense of shame in doing so. She watched him, but he did not raise his eyes to her face.

"Maybe tha should know, lad, that what is true of thy condition is true of Madeleine's too—at least, before she was assaulted by those thugs in the place where she came from. She'd not known a man before that day."

William sat quite still, taking this information in, his face quiet, betraying nothing now, listening to what she had to say.

"So neither one of the pair of you has learned the arts of love. People think 'tis only like the animals, it'll all come naturally. But I tell thee, lad, there's many a woman disappointed through that philosophy—and in the end a disappointed woman will make a disappointed man. The love between man and woman is only partly instinct. 'Tis also knowledge. If tha has thy chance (and why should tha not? I have prayed for thee), there are things tha will need to get right. All that Madeleine knows for herself, in her own body, of what is between man and woman is violence and fear. Tha'll have thy work cut out for thee to woo her to a place where she is not afraid and can welcome thee. And how can tha do that if no one's ever told thee how to please a woman, what to do?"

She paused and looked at him, but he made no reply, remaining silent and impassive, but not indifferent; waiting, alert to what she was telling him. So she continued, "I'm going to tell thee, then, what tha needs to know. If it's not knowledge tha needs ever, what's the harm? If it comes in handy, well, tha'll thank me when that night is done. Listen well, then—for it's in my mind that no other body is like to tell thee this.

"Before ever tha takes a woman to bed, tha must court her—not at the beginning only, when friendship grows into love; I mean every time, every evening tha holds out hope will come down with the nightfall to making love when the two of you retire to bed. Tha must make her laugh; tha must remember the endearments, the compliments; make her feel treasured, make her feel adored. Tha must woo her, find her eyes wi' thy eyes; tha must make love in a thousand ways before ever tha thinks of leading the way to the bedroom.

"Take time for conversation with her—women do not like to make love with strangers. The man who works all day, comes home, eats the dinner she's cooked, quaffs his ale, falls asleep and snores all evening, then turns to the woman handy in his bed to grab his rights and satisfy his wants need not be surprised to come home one fine day and discover she's left with the handsome gypsy who came to sell baskets at the door.

"Talk to her, lad; look at her, listen to her. And wash. She'll be hoping to find a man in her bed, not something like a lump of rancid bacon.

"Then, when it comes to the bedroom, here's four words tha should remember: patient and tender, light and slow. Hast tha got that? Patient and tender, light and slow. Love can be ardent and passionate, but not hasty or greedy or rushed.

"A woman wants to feel she has been taken reverently, like the host of God in the holy sanctuary, not torn apart and devoured like a hot roast bird on the kitchen table. Patient and tender, light and slow."

She went on to tell him with an explicit candor he found quite astonishing—and illuminating—of the techniques of love. She talked of the bodies and responses of women, about timing and finding the rhythm of love. She spoke of how to touch and kiss a woman to please her, as well as of trust and gentleness, of the etiquette of the bedchamber, its courtesies and kindness.

As she talked, her wheezy voice slow and her breathing difficult, he listened intently, never interrupting her or looking at her. Some of what she told him made him blush; he could feel his heart beating as he imagined what she described, and he hoped desperately that when she looked at him she would not see how her words stirred and aroused him. Then finally she had done.

"There. That's all I wanted to tell thee."

He sat in silence. Across the abbey court, the bell began to ring for None. He didn't move.

"I think tha must go, my lad. And I am tired now. Come again soon to see me; tha'rt a blessing to me."

But William did not move to go immediately. He remained exactly as he was, thinking over all she had told him, considering it and committing it to memory. Then he smiled at her, and there was something shy in his smile that she liked, not the cynicism that he used to hide behind.

"By my faith, mother! I'm lost for words. I hardly dare stand up. How can I thank you? Keep on praying for us. And if the chance ever comes my way, I'll remember what you told me. Glory! How could I possibly forget?"

He leaned across the table, and he took her hand and kissed it. "God keep you. I hope you feel better tomorrow. I'll come back and check on you as soon as ever I can. Thank you. Really, thank you. Nobody else in all the earth would have done that for me."

"Aye, well—there are gifts hiding in old age, but a body wants sharp eyesight to see them for what they are. One of the gifts of an old woman is the liberty to talk freely with a man. Take it as the gift of an old 'un—and may it be wisdom tha can put to good use one day."

"Yes. Amen. Bless you, dearest. See you soon."

Her eyes were bright with love for him as she watched him go. As he went into the choir for the office of None, Ellen Cottingham also took time to give thanks to God. She thanked him from her heart that as the evening of her life drew down to night and falling darkness, she had been given again the thing she had lost and longed for, the gift of a son.

William had never found the afternoon office especially gripping in either content or form. On this day his body was present in chapel, but his mind was entirely elsewhere. Sitting, standing, kneeling, he said and sang what he should, but his thoughts were filled with old Mother Cottingham's careful, comprehensive, and disquietingly vivid advice: "Patient and tender, light and slow."

He tried to imagine what he might be thinking about, but he couldn't quite make it come real. The materials for his imagination were not there. Very few people had touched him, held him, in the whole course of his life. Of his mother's touch he had vivid memories of being dragged by the wrist from places where he had hidden among the outbuildings, to be more easily and conveniently thrashed by his father in the house. He must have been quite small then, he supposed. He had known the kiss of peace—sometimes meant, more often not—with his brothers in community in different places over the years. He thought of John's touch, careful and serious, on burns and bruises. He thought of Michael's touch that always had a smile and kind words to go with it. And whenever he recalled it to mind he could feel again, as if it happened now, Tom's embrace of forgiveness steady and strong. But to make love with a woman? Her body would be very different, he thought, from a man's. And her touch would be different too. He tried, but he couldn't imagine it—though he remembered vividly enough what it had felt like to hold Madeleine in his arms and kiss her. So he simply stowed away in his heart the advice he had been given, all of it carefully heeded and memorized and none of it forgotten, in the small but stubborn hope that it would be of use one day. Or night.

As the community, reverent and faithful, observed the rite ordained for the office of None and concluded with the beautiful last prayer—"May the souls of the faithful departed, through the mercy of God, rest in peace"—William was thinking, "patient and tender, light and slow."

"Amen," he murmured with the others.

When the office had ended, he lingered on for a while in the stillness and peace of the church, resting his head against the wooden paneling at the back of his stall—but only lightly, because it was carved and therefore uncomfortable. He let his being float and his mind drift, hovering over the prospect Mother Cottingham's words had conjured in his imagination ...wishing...dreaming....He allowed his memory to wander back to the one precious hour that summer night when he had held Madeleine to him and kissed her ... and kissed her again. When he reflected upon their comprehensive inexperience in such things, he thought it had been very far from clumsy, and they had both done almighty well. Every moment of that hour was etched on his heart forever, and he revisited it with the most indescribable longing. He knew he should be doing something more constructive with his time, but he just couldn't bear, not quite yet, couldn't bear to let it go. And then it began to feel more like torture than reverie, and he thought he'd better stop. He couldn't have this, however much he wanted it, and if he tormented himself with it too long he thought he might go out of his mind. Nothing seemed more likely to bring him back to inescapable reality than a visit to the infirmary and Father Oswald.

During the same stretch of time William was sitting in the chapel thinking ... remembering ... imagining ... dreaming ... Abbot John was muttering expletives about some of the new accountability practices his new cellarer's assistant had instigated throughout the whole community. John had agreed to these readily, seeing that they would support thrifty habits and good stewardship of their resources—which were, after all, not their own but God's—but he had not thought through, at the time of giving his permission, what the impact of the changes on his own life might actually be.

Today he had to return to the checker a tally of what he had used and when—candles, firewood, wine for his guests, vellum, sealing wax, ink; the list seemed to go on and on and must be produced if he wanted to put in an order for new supplies. It was Brother Thomas's job really, but at this time of year his experienced help with the harvest was needed as well as appreciated. July had been a dry month in the main, but a few spectacular thunderstorms bringing torrential rain had flattened a not insignificant proportion of the grain crops in the fields. What remained now in September was precious, and this dry warm spell might be crucial in gathering it in. Tom had promised to call in after None, as John had guests in the evening, but from Terce to None he was up on the hill, hard at work in the fields.

Under pressure and feeling irritable, Abbot John took his wax tablet with the tally of items used across to the checker, intending to raise with William the question of how necessary this might really be. William was not there.

"God give you good day, Brother Ambrose." John felt he was beginning to understand the controlled restraint and formality he had often sensed in Father Peregrine. He wondered how often the careful courtesy had been pulled like a blanket over a muddled heap of frustrations and irritations, things left half done and gaining in urgency every minute.

"I have brought the tally of items we have used in the abbot's house. Where do you want me to leave it? I imagine Father William would like to see it, but the sun is strong on his table there at this time of day, and I have no intention of writing him another list if he can't read this because the wax has melted."

Brother Ambrose heard the asperity in his abbot's voice and held out his hand for the thing with a smile. "Leave it with me, Father."

"Thank you. Can I take another one, please? Father William has asked that I furnish you with a list of my known guests for the foreseeable future, so he can calculate the necessary extra supplies for the kitchen. Thank you. Where is he, by the way?"

Brother Ambrose chuckled. "Where's the wind? Blowing round the abbey causing trouble, I've no doubt. He was here earlier on, in more cheerful mood than mostly—oh, yes, that's where he'll be. Mistress Hazell was in here to see him this morning and said Mother Cottingham and Father Oswald both wanted to see him. He went directly after we ate to Mother Cottingham, so I suppose he'll have gone to see Father Oswald now. He said he would go."

John listened to this carefully. "Will you ask him to come and see me when he returns?"

Brother Ambrose had the impression his abbot was even more out of sorts when he left than when he came in. He wondered why, couldn't think of a reason, shrugged it off, and went back to work.

Madeleine meanwhile had made her way to the little parlor opening onto the abbey court adjacent to the abbot's house, to meet Father Theodore and make her confession. She had told him plainly and without reserve what had passed between her and William when she met with Theo a month ago in August. She had left the little oratory that summer day knowing how much she loved William and that he meant everything to her, but knowing as well that devious, covert love was not what she wanted. She could see the sense of discretion; she accepted reluctantly that if her brother got wind of this he would be placed in an impossible position, so he must never know. But her confessor sat in the room with her as the vicar of Jesus himself, and she would not deceive him, whether by what she said or equally by what she withheld.

Theodore had made no judgments. He had asked her questions, made sure she understood William's commitment as a professed brother and a priest—that this was in the same category as adultery because William had made his vows and was no longer free to change his mind. Did she know this? Yes, she did. He had asked her if they had plans to further the relationship. Had they arranged meetings? Had they made promises? How did things stand? And she had explained, and he recognized the sadness and weariness in her voice, that they knew they could not be together not only because of William's vows but because neither of them had anywhere else but this place to go. She expressed her sense of guilt and shame at concealing from her brother that they had met—and left Theodore in no doubt that William did not regard this concealment lightly either. She explained that William had said they must not meet, could not meet, that she was free to find another man for herself if she could, for he must not consort with her at all—both because it was not right and because it was too risky. "But there is nobody else in all the world I want," she had finished sadly.

Theodore half wished she had kept the information to herself but felt satisfied that he was dealing with two people who loved each other and had stolen one—well, two—forbidden encounters. He was not being made complicit in a secret elopement or clandestine affair. He thought the pain of separation probably penance enough; it certainly explained the misery that hung like a pall of dark smoke around William and his immoderate diligence and industry in the cellarer's work. Evidently he was running away from himself, without any success.

When she came to him again on this day in mid-September,

he hoped fervently that Madeleine had no further revelations of similar kind. By no word or look or any other indication would he have even considered betraying the secrets entrusted to him in the confessional, but he could not be any kind of accomplice to an affair between one of the monks and the abbot's sister.

She told him nothing of the conversation in the checker earlier that day. She was not sure if it was a sin. She was not sure if it was anything—at least, not anything wrong. To love someone, and long for them, and let them see that was how things were with you, surely that was not wrong? He was solemnly professed, but . . . in Madeleine's mind and, she thought, in William's as well, that was not really the same thing as being married to another woman. Who would be hurt by his loving her? God? Why? How? Or the community? More likely the community would be wounded by the suffering and festering of love suppressed that would not go away. She felt deeply conscious of the burden her confession in August must have laid upon Father Theodore; she saw no need to add to it today by relating tales of William teasing her with double entrendres and wooing her with the look in his eyes. They had been in plain sight. If Brother Ambrose was too obtuse to notice, whose fault was that?

Even so, Father Theodore's perceptive gentleness felt its way to her unhappiness—that nothing had changed for either of them, and they were living with it simply because they must. He thought it wiser not to allow this relationship to progress from the dominating feature to the defining reality of their lives, and so he moved on to asking her about her other friendships, her work with the villagers, and her practice of prayer as well.

He blessed her and absolved her, asking her to say her rosary and to keep those things that puzzled her or hurt her always honestly open before the loving face of Christ. And, after a moment's hesitation, he said he was grateful that both she and William cared enough about her brother and about the community and respected them enough to struggle against the love that had taken their hearts by storm. He assured her he would not fail in praying for the both of them, that their feet would find Christ's way of life for them.

Madeleine was not sure she had found anything like peace of mind in the confessional; she did not exactly leave feeling cleansed and renewed, but she knew she had made a good choice in her confessor. Rarely in her life had she met such a wise and compassionate soul, she thought.

On her way out of the parlor, her eye took in the strong circle of the sturdy protective walls and the open space of the abbey court, warm in the autumn sunshine, and she saw her brother emerging from the checker. Even at that distance she thought he looked cross. If she went straight back home as she'd intended, she would meet him returning to the abbot's house. She settled for an airy wave and a pretended errand in a completely different direction, walking the long way round by the fishponds, under the trees and past the stables to the abbey gate, and thence to Peartree Cottage in the close.

William, tearing himself from his private reverie in the choir, had gone out via the sacristy and vestry, through the door in the south wall near the Lady Chapel on his way to the infirmary. He never looked forward to his visits with Father Oswald. It had been at his instigation that the journey had been made to search for him and bring him back here to safety, and he felt glad they had done it. But Oswald, maimed and mutilated by those who hated him, blinded and with his tongue cut out, was a different proposition from Oswald as he had once been—the fastidious, refined aristocrat of elegant manners who had irritated William enough even then but had not revolted him with escaping streams of saliva and hawked-up boluses of food.

Conversation with him was arduous. The sign language of

the silence was designed for brief, practical communications—
"Look out, abbot's coming!" or "Pass me the fish," or "Give me
that breviary—no, the big one," and so on. It did not serve for
social conversation; that was never its intention. William found
that everything went better with Oswald if he just started talking and kept going, producing a flow of anodyne chatter about
his daily work and life around the monastery, leaving Oswald
to contribute as little as possible to the conversation. Having
been discouraged all his life from talking when he had nothing
to say—and even sometimes when he had—it did not come with
any facility to William now to muster a stream of idle chitchat
that would go on long enough to fill the best part of an hour. He
had to gather a significant level of resolve to leave the peace
of the chapel and set himself to make this overdue visit to the
infirmary.

The contrast dazzled him for a moment as he stepped out of
the dimness of the church into the sunshine. From nowhere, as
he momentarily stopped to let his eyes adjust, came a memory
from his first days in religion. His novice master, a peculiarly
sadistic man, quick to pass by the Hail Mary and Psalm 51 and
move on to the lash, had laid the scourge on him heavy for some
offense . . . what? William couldn't remember at this distance
of time. Insolence probably. Or arrogance. It was usually that.
Whichever, or whether it was both, he had been punished with
exceptional zeal and then given a hair shirt to wear because
they'd been coming into Lent. He remembered the shirt, driving him crazy, giving him no rest and exiling him from sleep,
prickling and irritating the stinging welts on his back until
. . . Standing there in the sunshine now, he shut the memory
down. But from underneath it slid one ghastly afternoon in
his childhood—a day as bright as this—when his mother had
dragged him in from playing in the yard to be punished for
some misdemeanor he'd forgotten even then, let alone now.
He was only a little boy. And seeing his father unbuckling his

belt and standing holding the strap end with the buckle end swinging free and realizing what he meant to do to him, he'd . . . William's mind recoiled dizzy with shame from the memory even now of the sudden simultaneous voiding of his bladder and bowels that had brought such a holocaust of wrath crashing down upon him as he could not bear to look back on.

He walked swiftly along the cobbled path that skirted the orchard and vegetable gardens and past the herbs (still attracting bees in good numbers) of the physic garden, trying to go faster than the memories that wanted entrance to his conscious mind.

But the thing was, though he had never worn a hair shirt again once he'd gained the status to refuse, Oswald's company itched and enervated him almost as fiercely as that chafing, excoriating garment he had been forced to put on. And the memory of the hair shirt set off the incursion of other memories, and he didn't want any of them.

Besides all of which, if he was honest with himself, he knew he neglected Oswald, who was lonely and eager for intelligent, friendly companionship. William felt guilty about it and ashamed of himself, until by the time he'd finished he almost hated Oswald and could hardly bear to go near him. And that brought fresh waves of shame as well. Shame and guilt, he thought—they fed on themselves.

So as he walked, deliberately he made himself notice everything, obstinately declining to look ahead to his visit with Oswald or search further than those sudden unsought glimpses of memory back into the horror chamber of his youth. He brought his mind to bear on the steadying reality of the exact present: that a few cobbles needed resetting, that some of the apples trees had been badly pruned, that the lavender bushes looked straggly now and needed cutting back, and that the hinge of the infirmary door had started a horrendous creak that probably meant it ought to be rehung and the hinges oiled.

Oswald was pitifully pleased to see him. Turning his sight-less face eagerly toward the sound of William's voice, he reached out to him, groping for the touch of his habit or his hand. William quelled firmly the unwanted sense of revulsion and reluctance that rose like nausea, and came in from the doorway of the room. He fetched the stool that stood in the corner there and placed it near Oswald—perhaps a yard away—before he stepped nearer to greet him. Then he grasped both those hands to stop their eerie feeling of the air. And impelled by a sudden, unexpected wrench of pity, he bent and kissed Oswald lightly on the forehead. The second he'd done it, he wished he had not. Oswald craved his company too ravenously as it was.

And then he regretted the silence he had permitted while he struggled with guilt and pity and shame and more guilt, because it gave Oswald the chance to ask him a question, and the less time he spent with him the less he understood his ruined speech. With a gentle squeeze of friendship, he with-drew his hands from Oswald's grasp and sat down on the stool he had set beside him.

"I'm sorry, you'll have to say that again," he said. And he knew the whole hour would go that way, and so it did.

He judged by the slant of the sun into the room, and not by his sense of time passing, when his visit had extended long enough. He had gossiped amiably of visiting tradesmen and delayed building works and techniques of extorting money from recalcitrant tenants. He made Oswald laugh (and steeled himself to merely lower his eyes and not physically turn his head away from that); he brought animation and interest and amusement to his brother's face.

And then, just when he judged it reasonable to take his leave, Oswald asked him, taking trouble to make his words as plain as he could, "And you? How are you?"

William was suddenly still. It occurred to him that if there was anyone you could trust with the burdens of your soul, it had to be a friend with his tongue cut out. His abbot was his confessor, but Oswald was as much a priest as John. This presented an opportunity to keep faith with his obligations as a monk without having to apprise John of the extent of his relationship with Madeleine.

"Father," he said softly, on impulse, "would you hear my confession?"

"Just a minute," he said and went and shut the door. Returning to sit at Oswald's side, he saw that his friend sat with compassion clear on his face, ready to hear his trouble. Something in him recoiled from the unwanted intimacy inherent in the interaction, but without allowing himself second thoughts, he took his seat again and told Oswald simply, briefly, holding nothing back, everything about himself and Madeleine. He felt palpitations of panic at what he was doing, but he told him of the agony of loving her and the dust and ashes that monastic obedience had become. He made no excuses, no attempt to justify himself. He did not describe in any detail what had happened in Madeleine's house that night in July or the sweetness of his stolen kiss in the oratory, but he did not leave those things out. "So I have betrayed my abbot and betrayed this house's kindness. I have betrayed my vocation and sinned against my God, and I could not confess it, for fear of being flung out. Will you . . . will you absolve me?"

He wished Oswald would just say the words of absolution and it would be done. Instead, Oswald asked him, painstakingly framing the words, "Have you let this love go?"

"What?" said William. It was completely incomprehensible. Oswald took his hand and asked the question again . . . and again . . . as he traced the letters of his words on William's palm.

"Oh," said William, light dawning. "No. No, I have not. I could sooner let my soul go and watch it fall to hell." He wondered with a sudden clutch of fright if that was in fact precisely what he'd done.

"What would you have forgiven?" Oswald traced *what for-give* on William's upheld palm.

William swallowed. "I cannot renounce it, Father," he said. "I cannot let it go. I am sorry that I had not the forbearance to hold it in my heart only. I'm sorry I went behind John's back to give physical expression to something neither Madeleine nor I can have. I'm sorry I could not wait in patience for something that almost certainly will never have its day, never come to me. I'm sorry for the lies and that I have to keep the truth concealed from John. I'm sorry for having created the situation. But I'm not sorry for the love."

Oswald released William's hand and groped for the beaker of drinking water that stood on the small table at his side. He dipped his fingers in it and shook the water in the general direction of his friend. *"Asperges me, Domine . . ."* He pronounced the absolution, and as he said the familiar if undistinguishable words, William's mind raced, in turmoil. What had he done? How safe would this information be? This man was lonely, and bored, and not completely incapable of speech. He tried to pay attention to the spiritual depth of what was happening and failed completely. But he took it in all seriousness and knew enough about Oswald's own history to be sure he would be neither shocked nor surprised.

"Would you give me penance?" he asked.

He could not understand Oswald's reply at all, and after another unsuccessful attempt, Oswald reached for his hand again.

William watched the finger of his brother trace the words on his palm: *Go . . . on . . . living.* Then Oswald folded William's hand shut and returned it to his lap. Evidently he thought the situation itself provided penance enough.

"Thank you, my brother," said William quietly. He wanted to secure Oswald's promise that he would keep this confidence, stress to him that not a hint of this must reach anyone, but he restrained himself. He would not stoop so low as to insult his brother, a priest of the church, with the suggestion that he might break the sacred silence of the confessional, even if he doubted his steadfastness as a friend. "Thank you. I must go now, but I'll come back soon." Even as he said the words he knew he'd added another lie to the ones from which Oswald had only just that minute absolved him. He would come back when he had to, when guilt pushed him to it, when he couldn't put off a visit any longer. And it was past what he could imagine of himself that he would come back sooner. The familiarity of shame at who he was settled round him as he made his farewell and finally walked away.

Anxiety fretted at him lest Oswald not keep his confidence. He knew Oswald well enough that it would not surprise him at all if he did not. He felt ashamed of his own insufficiency as a friend, his lack of charity as a monk, his cynicism as a man. He walked into the checker feeling thoroughly at odds with himself and the whole of the world.

Brother Ambrose looked up from the table over which he was bent, making up bundles of garden twine. "Oh—there you are, Father. Our abbot was looking for you. I said I'd send you over when you got back. Been at the infirmary?"

"Yes. What's the matter with him? Father John I mean."

Brother Ambrose perceived that the brief glimpse of sunshine he'd seen this morning had clouded over again.

"I think, Father—though I can't swear to it—that he's not as enamored of your system of lists and checks as you might have been hoping."

A quick grimace of exasperation flashed before William suppressed it. He sighed.

"Oh, all right—I'll go and find out what's wrong with him. Why not waste the tail end of the day? The rest of it's gone."

Meanwhile, in the abbot's house Brother Thomas had returned from his labors on the farm, pleasantly aching from hard work, tired and hungry enough to be looking forward to his supper and an evening with his feet up in conversation with his brothers.

"Day go well?" his abbot inquired, barely waiting for a reply before continuing. "Oh, I have yet *another* of these confounded lists—can you help me with it, please? I must learn to be a bit more methodical myself. I've got notes here and there. If you could take the tablet and the stylus and write down the guests as I tell you their names, I'll look through this pile of letters to check who's coming and when—I mean, I did send word to the guesthouse as each letter came in (or you did, to be accurate)—I can't see why Father William can't simply check with Father Dominic. Anyway, are you ready?"

Not without effort Tom resigned himself to a further demanding chore before the day could end. He obediently took the wax tablet and stood waiting with the stylus poised in his hand.

"Sir Geoffrey and Lady Agnes d'Ebassier are coming to visit for just a few days on their way to Scotland toward the end of this month, with all their retinue, so that's worth making a note of. Sometime during Advent there will be visits from the families of the lads in the novitiate—they're bound to want to come. But between Michaelmas and All Hallows there is no one much expected except the prior and novice master from St. Mary's in York who want to see Father Theodore and—"

"Hold on!" Tom interrupted him.

"What?"

"You're going too fast. I've only got as far as 'Sir Geoffrey.' I haven't even written down 'and Lady Agnes d'Ebassier' yet. By the time I get to the next one I'll have forgotten what you said. And . . . well, to be honest, I'm not that grand at writing. How do you spell 'Geoffrey'? I think it has more than one *f*, doesn't it?"

"What? Not 'Sir Geoffrey and Lady Agnes d'Ebassier' for mercy's sake!"

"But—that's who you said."

"Oh, God in heaven grant me patience! Look—Tom, you just write 'd'Ebassier.' Who else is it likely to be? Holy saints, this is going to take up the whole of the rest of the day! Never mind—just give it to me; I'll do it myself. Give it to me! No, truly!"

Looking more than a little hurt, Brother Thomas surrendered the tablet to his superior, then he heard a quick, sharp knock on the door from the abbey court, and he knew who that was.

William did him the courtesy of a quick glance and a nod as he came into the room and gave his attention to the abbot.

"You asked to see me?" His tone was brusque.

Here we go, thought Brother Thomas, *flint on flint*.

"I am cumbered about by your confounded lists!" John stood with the tablet in his hands, wishing the only thing written on it was not a misspelling of Sir Geoffrey. "I got rid of the last blasted list to the checker this morning, only to find myself saddled with the task of making another one—of every guest I can think of who's ever likely to visit me between now until I die or Christ comes again."

"Oh. How far have you got?"

He held out his hand for the tablet. John moved his thumb to cover the name and pressed it down hard and kept it there.

"I haven't got anywhere with it. I've only just started. It may amaze you to know this, but I do have some other things to do. Brother Thomas tells them at the guesthouse every time we hear someone will be coming. Can't you go and infest them with your infernal plague of lists?"

William's eyes flickered as he regarded his abbot in silence, and that annoyed John even more.

"Well?"

"But you agreed—" William tried to sound more patient than he felt.

"I know I did!" John snapped back. "And I can't have been

thinking straight! You can take your wax tablets and shove 'em up—" He stopped abruptly.

Brother Tom turned away from this conversation and occupied himself with some pointless activity that required him to bend down to the hearth. If either of them saw his amusement, he thought the consequences could be dire.

"Oh, dear, I'm sorry, brother." John made himself speak more calmly. "It just makes so much more work out of every blessed thing."

A thunderous knocking at the cloister door made all three of them jump.

"*Mater Dei!* For heaven's sake! What *now*?"

Before Brother Tom could rise to answer it, Abbot John was across the room and had the door yanked open. "Whatever do you think you're doing, brother? Does 'quiet' mean anything to you? What are you trying to do? Knock the door down or raise the blessed dead?"

Chastened, Brother Benedict, who stood on the step, smote his breast. "*Mea culpa.* But Father, please—can you come—I can't find Brother Michael and I think Father Oswald is dead."

It took only a split second for his abbot to gather his wits, in which time Brother Thomas had taken the tablet and stylus out of his unresisting hands.

Abbot John had worked in the infirmary all his adult life. When a matter of life and death was brought before him, he did not delay to discuss it or ask any questions. Lifting his hand to the novice's shoulder to turn him round, he set him off along the cloister as he stepped forward to accompany him.

"Father William," he said as an afterthought, looking back, "do you want to come with us?"

William did not. The thought of it made him feel queasy, but he followed them nevertheless.

"I'm so sorry," John said as he strode along beside the novice. "Forgive my impatience, Brother Benedict—I was rude to you. You can tell me what's happened as we go."

By the time they reached the infirmary, Brother Michael was already kneeling by Father Oswald's body on the floor where it had fallen. What had happened was simple and not unexpected. The men in the infirmary took their supper before the rest of the community, to allow the brothers who worked there the opportunity to eat with the others in the frater later on. Brother Michael had gone outside in haste to get their washing in before the damps of the evening undid the good work of the afternoon sunshine. This left Brother Benedict and Martin, their assistant from the village, to serve the suppers. Three of the old men in the infirmary needed spoon-feeding and could not drink without help. Father Oswald could look after himself, though supervision was advisable. He had mastered the art of eating remarkably well, but the danger of choking remained an ever-present threat.

And this time he had lost the battle—in the few minutes that Michael attended to the washing and Benedict and Martin fed mashed beans and gravy and rich red wine, with gentle patience, to the frail and ancient inhabitants under their care.

It would have taken only a few short minutes. Martin heard him choking and thought little of it; Father Oswald needed to hawk and cough his way through every meal. Then he heard the crash of him falling and the chair and table falling, too, and the bowl and beaker smashing as they hit the ground. He left what he was doing, put his head round the door, panicked, and called out for Brother Benedict, who had come at a run but didn't know what to do. The sight of Father Oswald, his hands to his throat as he fought ineffectually for breath, his face contused purple and his body thrashing on the ground, frightened them both.

Brother Benedict told Martin to find Brother Michael at once, and he was glad to leave in obedience to this instruction.

The novice had found the courage to pick his way through the wreckage and kneel by the choking, writhing body, trying (without success) to tip him forward. He gave him an experimental thump on the back, which made no difference at all. He hit him again, harder, and harder again, and Father Oswald fell limp. Relieved, Brother Benedict thought he had solved the problem at first. But when he spoke Oswald's name, no response came. Terrified then, he turned the man's head so he could see his face. Purple still, it sagged unresponsive. It was hard to tell, partly because he had never seen a dead man before and partly because Father Oswald had no eyes, but Brother Benedict thought he might be dead. Without waiting to see if Martin had found Brother Michael, he scrambled to his feet and did the only thing he could think of. He ran for Father John.

Abbot John did not run, but he put on a fair turn of speed as he walked along the path to the infirmary. William kept his pace with ease, but Brother Benedict had to trot.

They arrived at the doorway of Oswald's room to find Michael kneeling at Oswald's side checking for signs of life, but it was evident that help had come too late. John stopped in the doorway, the other two men behind him. He turned to the novice. Benedict's face looked pale and pinched with fear. He felt responsible.

"Brother Benedict," John said kindly and calmly, "please go and satisfy yourself that Martin has the other men's suppers in hand and all the feeders have been cared for. Then get a brush, rags, and a pail of soapy water to clean up in here. There's no call for you to reproach yourself about this. It was waiting to happen. Truly, it could only be a matter of time. We gave Father Oswald some months of peace and dignity here, but there were some things we could not do. Please don't blame yourself. It was not your fault."

The novice nodded gratefully and hurried to make amends for his ineptitude by supervising whatever of supper still waited to be done. John looked at William, appraising his state of mind.

"You don't have to come in," he said. "There is nothing but a body in here."

"Thanks!" said Brother Michael over his shoulder.

That made them both smile, and William felt an obligation to face this moment. He followed John into the room.

Brother Michael, having assured himself there were no vital signs and death was certain, now got to his feet and picked up the table. Abbot John lifted up the chair. Its cushion was in among the debris of broken crockery and splashed food and drink, so for the moment he let it lie.

As the two of them set the room to rights, William knelt down beside his friend. With the side of his thumb he signed Oswald's forehead with the cross of Jesus. He murmured a prayer of blessing, commending his soul to God, and a *Pater Noster*, an *Ave Maria*, and a *Gloria*. Brother Michael and Abbot John stopped what they were doing and stood in the silent reverence of this farewell as he made his prayer. "God bless you, Oswald," whispered William finally. "May Christ receive you in heaven, and may God have mercy on your soul. May your soul be held safe this day in the hands of God, and there may no torment touch you ever again."

He sat back on his heels and stared soberly down at Oswald's dead face. As he looked at its purple contusion, it occurred to him that without Brother Tom's swift and clearheaded action earlier in the year, the fallen body of death on the floor might have been himself. In this moment he had no idea at all what he thought about that. He reflected that whatever else an end may be, it offers a solution.

"Let's lift him onto the bed." Abbot John's quiet voice recalled him. William got to his feet, out of their way, watching his abbot and Brother Michael lift the corpse with practiced ease onto the bed they had just stripped of blankets to receive it.

"Shall we do it together?" asked Abbot John. Michael smiled at him, nodding his assent. It felt good to work as a team again on this sacred task of washing and laying out the blessed dead.

Brother Benedict returned with his bucket and rags and brush. William saw that at this point he became nothing more than part of the clutter. He thanked John for letting him come and make his farewell, then slipped away.

He had lost track of the time, and he didn't want to go back to the checker. He walked back along the path for the second time that day, reminded himself to speak to someone about fixing those cobbles, went into the church through the Lady Chapel and then to the choir. It surprised him to find men gathering quietly for Vespers. He had not grasped that he'd missed supper, and he didn't feel hungry. He wondered how long he'd knelt by Oswald's body. Such a curious thing, so uneven—the passing of time.

Seeing Father Chad in his stall, William crossed the chapel to speak to him. The prior sat in silent meditation, his eyes closed in prayer.

"Father Chad."

The prior's eyes snapped open as William spoke his name in the softest undertone.

"Yes? Is something amiss?"

"Father Abbot is detained. Father Oswald has died—very suddenly. Father John is with Brother Michael in the infirmary now. It may be that you will have to stand in for him for Vespers. Or he may come. I don't know."

As the prior got to his feet with an air of importance, William thought that few things irritated him as much as Father Chad rising to the occasion. He bent his head in a small bow of submission and went back to his own seat.

Around the chapel, he saw men taking note with the slightest lifting of the head or movement of the eyes that Father Chad sat in the abbot's place, which signaled some event must have disrupted the routine.

William sat in his stall, finding the place in the breviary. The silence of the church was more underlined than disturbed by the quiet sound of individuals making their way into the choir. He lifted his cowl over his head and folded his hands inside his sleeves. He felt a momentary impulse of gratitude that Brother Robert had not yet arrived. That novice seemed to find him irresistibly intriguing and watched him most of the time. The only refuge of privacy lay in closing his eyes. For now he let his gaze wander, loving the holiness and austerity of this place of prayer.

The quiet settled around him, and he thought back over the afternoon. By hindsight he considered his decision to confide in Father Oswald to have been seriously foolish. He did not believe Oswald would have directly betrayed his confidence, but the more he reflected on it, the more sure he felt that somewhere, somehow, something would have leaked out and Oswald would have been the source.

Thank God. Oh, thank God, his heart whispered as he sat in the stillness and tried to prepare himself for devotion. Brother Robert slid into his place. William closed his eyes. He felt appalled to find in his heart not one vestige of grief for Oswald's passing—this brother with whom he'd traveled the monastic way for upward of two decades. He could feel only desperate relief that this afternoon's impulsive indiscretion had been given no time to germinate in Oswald's mind and begin to push its way up to the light and the open air. Relief, too, that Madeleine had reminded him of his duty to make that visit— otherwise now he would be even more harrowed with guilt than he already was.

And he wondered, facing the fact that he felt so heartily glad Oswald was dead, if it might be possible for a man to be so engulfed in guilt and shame at his private thoughts that he lost himself forever.

As he looked at the mess of his life, he saw only one candle of hope still shining. In the spring of the year, during Lent, he had made a financial transaction on his own initiative that he felt fairly certain, added together with the unremitting hard work he had put in through the course of the summer, would bring the community back into robust fiscal health. As he thought about himself, his relationships and responses, this began to feel like the one redeeming feature of his life.

The tolling of the bell slowed and ceased. The prior's ring knocked on the wood of the abbot's stall. With a wave of subdued sound, the robed community rose as one.

"Deus in adjutorium meum intende."

They responded, *"Domine ad adjuvandum me festina."*

"Oh, God, come to my assistance. Oh, Lord, make speed to save me." *Oh... yes, please* . . . William's heart pleaded silently as the brothers' voices rose in prayer.

111

CHAPTER
FOUR

October

Brother Paulinus's heart always gave a little lurch of excitement when one of his homing pigeons returned. They never failed to come back. Brother Paulinus loved his garden, and he loved the birds and would spend patient hours with them, crooning softly to them, gentling and befriending them until they would perch on his finger and he could do anything with them. Birds that have a sense of kinship will always come home, flying amazing distances through all weathers to the place where they belong.

The one that came back today was a sturdy grizzle hen who would fly as far as was asked of her. Brother Paulinus, working out in the garden, watched her sail down, wings outspread, and stretched out his right hand like Noah, offering her a perch to land on.

She had been taken way back in Holy Week. William de Bulmer had asked for a bird to send south with a London merchant with whom he'd done business on Maundy Thursday. Brother Paulinus privately took a very dim view indeed of anyone doing business on Maundy Thursday, but he understood that the cellarer's work was unarguably fraught with challenges, so he chose to take a charitable attitude. He had given William the grizzle hen, with strict instructions as to her care, and had seen no more of her again for these last six months, but now on this October morning she had returned. He took the bird into the security of the pigeon loft, removed with care the message she carried, and went with it to Father William in the checker. William thanked him, took it eagerly, and read it; then his face went as white as a sheet. For a few moments he sat quite still; then, abruptly, without a word of explanation, he left his table at the checker and, with the rolled scrap of parchment bearing the message still held in his hand, walked out of the door. Brother Paulinus and Brother Ambrose looked at each other. Brother Ambrose shrugged. "Nowt so queer as folk!" he exclaimed. "No doubt we'll be hearing soon enough what the matter is."

In the course of learning the craft of a physician, John had grown to recognize a particular look of desperate courage on a man's face: he'd seen it in the eyes of a man waiting to have his foot amputated; of another receiving confirmation that the pox he'd caught would take his sanity first and his life afterward; of another who had just taken off his tunic so the surgeon could cut out a tumor; of another called into the room where his new-born son and the child's mother lay both dead. He'd even seen it on the face of a novice—a delicate boy of aristocratic blood, barely eighteen years old—caught in some misdemeanor and required to strip to his breeches and kneel to be thrashed with the scourge in Chapter. John had long forgotten the offense, but he remembered the look on the boy's white face. He had seen that look so many times over the years, and he realized he could see it in William's face now.

He addressed himself to the fear that lay behind it before he inquired as to the cause.

"Sit you down," he said gently, and he closed the door. He came to sit opposite William. "What's amiss?"

He saw that William was trembling, his face completely gray. In his hands he clutched a small scrap of parchment.

John waited, but William did not speak; he just sat, shaking and looking down at the scrap of vellum. Then he buried his face in his hands.

John moved from his chair, came and squatted by William, rested his hand on William's knee. "For the love of God, brother—whatever is it? What's happened?"

Tense and shaking, his face hidden in his hands, William did not attempt to speak. Perplexed, John waited a while longer, then drew the scrap of parchment out from between William's fingers, a tiny square that had been rolled and sealed.

He held it flat to read what had been written there, in neat, cramped script: "Got home but storm at the last. Blown onto rocks at Lizard Point. Lady Eleanor is lost." Putting out a hand to steady himself on the arm of William's chair, John stood up. He looked down at William, still puzzled.

"What is this?" he said. "Who is Lady Eleanor? Is this a relative? This has come with a carrier pigeon? William, speak to me. It will only be a matter of time before someone else is battering at my door. Who is Lady Eleanor?"

"Not 'who,'" William replied, his voice husky, willing himself to lower his trembling hands to his lap. He sat hunched, his head bowed. "'What.' *Lady Eleanor* is a ship. I think I have just ruined us."

John sat down, very quietly, and gave William his full attention. "Please explain."

He did not need William to say how utterly wretched he felt; John could see it plainly. His hands gripped hard together, his voice low, his head bent, William told him what had come to pass.

"On Maundy Thursday there came a merchant with the pilgrims here. I was looking for traders because we had a lot of things that needed sorting out. Columba was holy, and a good abbot—a wonderful man for the care of souls—but there had been too much cheeseparing; he was holier than the abbacy can stand. And Ambrose is good, and faithful, but he is old. He is not decisive, and has not a very tight grip on . . . anything.

"We were short on essential things in every place—the infirmary, the sacristy, the robing room, the kitchens, the guesthouse, the scriptorium. Wherever I looked, I found work could not proceed because we were wanting salt for preserving, or spices for embalming, or pigments for inks, or sturdy cloth for robes, or silver and ivory and fine hides for the books that will bring us a good price. The buildings are all in good repair, but that's the best can be said—and much of that due to Brother Thomas and Brother Stephen—dedicated hard work and skilled hands.

"This man—this merchant—had an offer to make us that seemed too good to refuse. His ship, the *Lady Eleanor*, had gone out last year, overwintered, and was on her way home. She was loaded with everything we wanted. Bolts of woolen cloth for habits and silks for altar frontals—ours are in a scandalous condition. She had sandalwood, attar of rose, myrrh, frankincense, spikenard, ambergris—all the aromatics we are short of in the infirmary, and also the resins: frankincense and myrrh from Araby. We have ample incense right now, but we can sell it on at a profit any time we choose. She had cinnamon, cloves, nutmeg, allspice, saffron, ginger, mace—and the white sage for burning also, which we cannot usually get for love nor money. There was cassia and anise, too, marjoram and cumin. They had dried fruit—raisins, dates, figs and prunes, along with almonds aplenty, and rice. They'd olive oil and good wine—sacramental grade. They'd stopped in Venice and taken on glass and silver. I don't know if you're aware, but silver is rising steadily in price because the Venetians are bent on buying up all of it, and it's becoming so costly. To get some that has been already bought before the prices go sky-high seemed prudent. They had come back leisurely, trading all the way, and they had on board the store cupboard of our dreams. They were stopping at Bruges for lace. They even planned to sail round to Ireland for some fair linen before finally coming into the Thames estuary, and then up the east coast to Scarborough with the goods we had asked for. They had also coarse linen—they had pepper, they had nutmeg, they even had some horses and a certain amount of marble. Bits from everywhere—and answering so many of our own needs.

"The original idea had been to call at ports along the south and east coasts, trading as they went. But they—the man who owned the ship—had run out of money and needed to send out his next trading vessel before the monies would be in from the *Lady Eleanor* coming home. He was looking for someone who would pay up front for what he had to offer, and in return he would cut the prices of everything paid for by a good margin. There was a risk, of course: buying goods unseen from a vessel not yet safely home, especially as there was no guarantee she would be safely docked before the autumn tides and storms. She was on her way back though, and if I took this chance it meant we could have, before the end of the year, the things we needed to get to work and earn our living, instead of tinkering about keeping ourselves occupied and making do. We have men of such talent and skill here. We do Christ no service to restrict what their hands can do by giving them no materials to work with. So I struck the deal."

John frowned. "You mean—you paid him?"

"Yes. I paid him."

"How much?"

"The best part of five hundred pounds."

For a moment John stopped breathing.

"We had it in store," said William. "I had been round the farms and taken in a substantial amount in tardy rents still held over from last Michaelmas. Money was owed us here and there by a considerable number of people from our scribing and bookbinding and illumination work. I got it in. I knew that once the Lady Day rents were in and some more hardheaded agreements than previously reached over the work of the scriptorium and the school, we could recoup enough money at least for the next round of papal taxes; and we don't have a visitation from the bishop until the spring. We'd be all right provided we had no unexpected demands from the Crown this year. And with what the five hundred pounds bought us, not only would our own stores be replenished for a long while to come, but we'd have the means to earn better than we presently do. So I gave him what we had—just about everything. I think we had about five pounds, eight shillings, and three farthings left in the chest once I paid him. I got a receipt."

"Did you consult Ambrose over this?"

William shook his head. "No. I didn't need to. I know what Ambrose would have thought. He would have thought it too risky and been horrified. Pirates. Rocks. Storms."

"Did you ask Father Chad?"

William looked at him with a certain measure of disbelief. "No. That didn't occur to me."

"So—you didn't ask any of us. You decided to gamble five hundred pounds—being the entire wealth of a monastery where you'd only just been admitted. And our annual income is—?"

"A hundred and eleven pounds, fifteen shillings, and sixpence. But after you take off the extra land we rent and various fees and such, last year we netted ninety-five pounds, twelve shillings, and tuppence—but that was before I got involved. I had it in mind that we can double that next year with increased output and what is owed us being chased up and coming in as it should."

"So . . . it would take us five years on present income to replace what we have lost."

"No. It will take us far, far longer than that because we have lost not only the money but the goods we needed to earn anything at all. And our earnings at under a hundred pounds a year only just about keep body and soul together; it goes out as fast as it comes in. Without an increase in income—and with no means now *to* increase our income—we can probably not even keep afloat, let alone claw back what we have lost. I meant what I said: I think I have ruined us. We are completely cleaned out, and we have nothing in store."

Abbot John sat transfixed, so many things going through his mind. He was appalled that William could have made free with what was not his to take. He was horrified that William had simply disregarded the absolute requirement not to act on his own initiative but always within the community's framework of authority; this was not merely to safeguard the stability of the house but was part of the discipline of life for a monk. It was part of the renunciation of worldly goods: no more bright ideas; no more self-aggrandizement; no more self-will or disregard of others. William knew that; every monk did. Explicit in the holy Rule in black and white, Benedict insisted that a cellarer make no decision on his own initiative alone but act always with the permission of his abbot. He would have to take William to task for his outrageous disobedience at some point, but this did not feel like the moment for scoldings—besides which he thought if the lesson had not been learned after this, it probably never would be. As the implications raced through John's mind he wondered what the responses of the brethren might be. He wondered if he would lose their confidence now, for good. It had been on his urging and entreaty that they consented to accept William—against their own better judgment—into their midst. He knew that Brother Ambrose's mind was frankly unequal to this dilemma. He knew that his own inexperience could offer no help—and his prior was likely to be a positive hindrance. With reluctance he came to the conclusion that the only man with half a chance of getting them out of the predicament they were in was the man who got them into it in the first place.

"So what do we do?" he asked simply.

Curious, relieved, William looked at him. John saw him fractionally relax.

"Is that all you're going to say to me?" he asked.

John shrugged. "I cannot think of anything to say that you do not already know full well. What has landed in our laps here is more important than any indignation of mine or remorse of yours. There remains a community to consider, and many who depend upon us. I'm afraid we have to fix this, and that won't be accomplished by recriminations and apologies. I think we have to come up with something, fast. Who else knows about this?"

"Nobody."

"You gave away *five hundred pounds* from our coffers and nobody *noticed*? What was Ambrose doing? Dozing?"

William shook his head.

"It was Holy Week, Father. We were all so busy, I should think Ambrose was meeting himself coming back. And besides that, I went through our accounts like a whirlwind, and I made inventories of everything. By Holy Thursday, if Brother Ambrose had seen me haul out our chests and empty the money into bags, he would hardly have raised an eyebrow. I could have sold the entire abbey out from under his feet and he'd never have noticed."

"Is there any possibility of getting some of our money back?"

"No. That was the deal we struck. I listed what I thought would benefit us from what they expected to have on board once they had completed the voyage, bearing in mind their last stops would be in Ireland and then in Bruges. I gave the money for what was on our list, with the agreement that those items were then ours. The goods came cheap, but they were ours—so, our risk. Everything on the list was ours both to have and to lose."

"But . . . if they were wrecked off Lizard Point, presumably they never made it to Bruges. And how do we know the rest of the items were even on board for sure, with such a mixed cargo?"

"You're right about Bruges. I think I can argue the point to get back the money for the lace—if he ever comes near us again—but the rest is known. They had their own carrier pigeons, same as us. The captain was able to send home reports at each stage. Apart from the Irish linen, when I saw the man in Holy Week he was able to show me a full inventory and let me choose from that."

"What do we want lace for anyway?"

"The sacristy. Some of our altar linen has almost had it. And Father James's stitching is exquisite. And Madeleine can embroider. I thought she might be glad to do a little work for us since she lives on our charity—she regards herself as part of the community in a way, I think. It was in my mind that we could produce some high-quality vestments and sanctuary linens if we had the materials. Anyway, never mind that, it's all gone now."

"God in heaven, William! What are we to do?"

"Well . . . we have no more cottages spare in the close, and because Chad filled up all the ones Columba had left empty, that means they're relatively new tenants, so no chance of any revenue from there for years—only obligations to maintain the houses and supply provisions according to each agreement. I think I have only two suggestions to make. It is possible we could ask Sir Geoffrey d'Ebassier for a loan. He might stump up two hundred pounds. No guarantee, but we can ask. Then the other thing we can do is offer corrodies instead of regular tenancies on perhaps three of our farms. If we tell them we shall be raising the rents next year, that should bait the hook, because if they'll buy a corrody of five years duration, that means they'll have pegged their rents and have five years immunity from increases. We could try the same thing with the school. They're paying two pounds a year at present; we could give them a choice between an increase to two guineas a year or a down payment for the whole five years at the present rate. Of course it also means we'll raise capital but lose income, which is never good news in the long term. It'll serve to get us out of a hole now, that's all.

"'We can always do nothing—just kiss it good-bye. That means some very lean, hand-to-mouth years scratching along with no reserves, unable to restock our supplies. We'll have to live with the frustration of able men with no materials to work with, but . . . " William shrugged. "It's an option. It's what Columba would have done, if that helps you make up your mind."

John looked at him thoughtfully, weighing these possibilities in his mind.

"Or we could sell pardons," said William as an afterthought.

"Are you serious? That business stinks."

"Surely it stinks, but where there's muck there's money."

John shook his head. "No. If we have to beg on the streets, we can do so with dignity and with our integrity intact. If we start selling pardons, the first thing we sell is our souls. We just become scum, exploiting people's terrors for our own gain. Not a pretty trade. Cross that one off your list."

William sat in concentrated thought for a little while longer, then spoke. "Leave it with me," he said. "I'll come up with something. I promise you I will. I'll get us out of this hole somehow."

"Well," John replied, "do your best, for we'll have to bring this before the community at Chapter in the morning."

William nodded, mute, gazing at nothing. That prospect seemed too appalling to be faced.

☥   ☥   ☥

Slowly he rose to his feet, and slowly he moved into the space at the center. He hated that yawning space at the center of the chapter house. He looked as though he could hardly put one foot in front of the other, his body tense and hunched. His face was ghastly pale and beset with tics and twitches. Standing before them, John saw he was shaking. Everyone saw it. The room became very still; no one moved, except Theodore, who leaned forward in his seat, a look of concern on his face. William licked his lips. Shaking violently, he tried several times to speak, but no sound would come out. Desperately, he raised his eyes to his abbot, so John explained, in calm and neutral terms, what had happened. That years of living very frugally had brought them out of debt, leaving them with the fabric of the buildings in excellent order but with a serious shortage of materials for the work of their hands whereby they might consolidate future security. That an excellent opportunity had arisen to purchase everything they needed at low cost from a vessel nearly home—with a risk therefore, but a relatively low risk. That there had been no need to go into debt to make this transaction, but it had used up reserves entirely, thus creating the probability of necessary debt in the likely event of demands from the Church or the Crown. That the intention had been to create an invigoration of earnings, thus replacing the reserves, increasing reputation and future prosperity and stability. That unfortunately the vessel, almost home, had gone down with all still aboard off the treacherous territory of England's southwest coast. That a great sum of money had therefore been lost, along with the goods implied. There was silence when John finished speaking. William looked as though he could barely stand.

"But . . . why . . . how . . . Father—why did you not consult me about this?" Old Brother Ambrose sounded hurt as well as amazed.

"Nor me!" exclaimed Father Chad. "I would never have endorsed such a suggestion! I do wish you had asked us, Father!"

John looked at him. "I didn't know either," he said quietly.

William bent his head. There are levels of silence. The

silence of the community entered a new depth as they grasped what had happened.

Again William licked his lips and tried to say he was sorry, but not even a whisper would come out. Still shaking, he knelt, his face to the floor, in the center of the room before them.

"So. What's to be done?" asked Brother Cormac.

This was easier for Abbot John to say. He felt a relief of tension as he outlined the two options: raising corrodies on some farms and borrowing from wealthy benefactors, or simply accepting several very lean years.

Brother Thomas asked to speak. His abbot nodded.

"Father, I'm sorry to go back to Father Peregrine—I know it can't feel easy for you—but I'm asking myself what he would have done. I've never had a great head for finance, and I didn't always listen properly to what he said because I couldn't take it in. But something once stuck in my mind, and I can only think I remember it because it was one of the last coherent things he ever did say. It was in the days before he was taken ill, when he sat up night after night the whole night long, working with the accounts to find a way through. I begged him to take some rest, but he would not. He was satisfied in the end that he had found a way to fulfill all we had to do without going into debt. He would not borrow; he would not raise the rents beyond what was at least fair and at best kind. And the thing I remember him saying, when there was a suggestion of selling corrodies, was: 'For years I labored to reclaim this abbey from its debts. I am not now going to encumber it with unwanted inhabitants mingling with the brothers to their spiritual detriment and weighing around our necks forever, just to raise ready money now.' That's what he said, and I remember it—if that helps any with finding a way forward."

Abbot John nodded. "Thank you. That's probably helpful. Corrodies do not need to be for life, of course. What we—this was William's suggestion—had in mind was a number—say,

three or four—of five-year corrodies raised on farms, in con-
junction with a modest increase in rents. That would give an
incentive to take up the offer of a corrody in order to (in effect)
peg the rent for five years. That gives us capital but exacerbates
our paucity of income. But our cottages, for good or ill, are now
filled. The corrodies we are talking about would not bring more
folk into the abbey. There's nowhere else outside the cloister to
put anybody."

"We must follow the way of frugality and simplicity," said
Brother Paulinus. " That's always the wisest course in the end.
These other solutions sound clever, but they bring unforeseen
trouble, and they make us vulnerable."

Several murmurs of assent followed those words.

"Father, might we be able to start small?" asked Francis.
"What I mean is, William seems to have identified a real problem with what we're doing. Basically he thought—presumably—that if we could be a bit more enterprising we have it
within us to prosper better than we do now. Well, we've lost
whatever it was on that ship—spices I guess, and aromatics,
incense and cloth and stone and pigments, and all that we've
been limping along without—but we can still adopt the prin-
ciple with what we do have to hand. We can season our food
with our own herbs and make hedgerow medicines of our own.
We can make pots from English clay bought at low prices and
sell our honey and our fruit. We can work on improving our
wine and use what inks we have to make what books we can to
raise some money. Just because we can't do everything doesn't
mean we can't do anything to improve. If we accept the frugality path, but make a pact with ourselves to work our way up to
something better, and if we pray, at least we aren't in debt, and
thank God for that."

Abbot John liked the sound of this, and the quiet affirma-
tions around the room showed this to be generally true. Father
Gilbert stood to say he had been approached before by young

men wanting to study music but had never taken it up; it would be a possibility. Brother Clement said their stores were very low, but if their efforts were to be directed at earning money rather than producing books for the community for a year, that might help. He also pointed out that they had some rare original texts in their library that could be sold for a goodly sum after copies had been made so their content would not be lost— a valuable book of the sermons of Aelred of Rievaulx, written and bound in his own hand, for example.

John felt surprised and heartened by the unexpectedly positive mood of the discussion. He could see an eagerness in the men's faces as they thought about what they individually could contribute. Then Theodore raised his hand. "Father, may I speak?"

John gestured to him to continue.

"These responses are encouraging and hopeful, and thank God for that; but aren't we forgetting something? Here's this poor man, so terrified of us he couldn't speak and could hardly even stand up, crouched here before us apparently completely forgotten. Financial stability is important, but it isn't everything. Might we put our mind to the man before we begin to think about the money?"

As his eyes met Theodore's, *I love you*, John thought; *you are Christ's man*.

"Indeed," he said. "Father William? Can you speak to us?"

William raised himself up to speak, still kneeling, still bent low. "I'm sorry," he said. "I'm so very, very sorry. I beg your forgiveness, my brothers, and I beg God's forgiveness. I should never have acted in so froward a manner. I should never have been so rash and arrogant. Or so stupid. I . . . I . . . I wanted to please you. To bring something of good to make up for . . . oh, God, I'm so desperately sorry . . . "

He spoke low, and the community had to listen intently to hear what he said. Out of the corner of his eye John caught a glimpse of Brother Paulinus's face screwed into a grimace as, deaf these days, he struggled to catch the words.

John looked at William and wondered whatever kind of penance he was supposed to give him. He observed that William was still trembling. He got up from his seat and moved to where William knelt. "You are forgiven, brother," he said. "God forgives you, and we forgive you. Everyone makes mistakes. But please, in future, will you remember to consult and to seek permission. You are a member of a community, and that has its strictures as well as its comfort."

He bent down and raised William up. "Take your seat, my brother," he said very quietly. "It's not all right, but it is forgiven."

His head bent so he didn't have to look at anybody, William made his way back to his stall and sat there bowed in shame while the discussion continued. A way forward was agreed upon unanimously: no borrowing; no more corrodies; determined austerity and new efforts and productivity and trade. Abbot John asked Brother Ambrose and Father Chad to meet with him and William in the abbot's house after the midday meal that day to look at the detail of implementing the community's decision.

The mood was optimistic as the men filtered out of the chapter house. William stayed where he was. Theodore came to stand before him, but William did not look up. "You'll get through it," said Theo gently, "we all do." He put out his hand and rested it on William's shoulder for a moment before he went on his way.

Eventually, when he judged that everyone had gone, William rose to his feet and walked slowly to the door. He did not know what he felt. He felt nothing. It was as though shame and failure had engulfed him and broken him and left him nothing. He felt his body moving of its own accord as though it no longer had a soul. He was lost now. He was nothing.

As he went through the doorway, he caught sight of a pair of sandaled feet. Startled, he looked up to see Brother Thomas leaning against the wall, waiting for him. Tom moved to block his path, and for a moment William's vision blurred and his throat closed in terror. He did not take in the expression on Tom's face, only the size and bulk of him standing there.

"Oh, you prize idiot!" said Tom and enveloped him in a hug. "For mercy's sake, what did you think I was going to do to you?" Shaking and faint, William gratefully allowed Tom's strength to hold him. "Oh God, I'm so sorry, Brother Thomas," he whispered, "I'm so sorry." And Tom just held him, thinking nothing but that this seemed to be his own principal contribution to the life of the community.

✠   ✠   ✠

As Abbot John made his way back along the cloister to his lodging after Chapter, Brother Dominic caught up with him to remind him that Brother Cassian's parents were coming to visit and would be hoping to hear from the abbot how their son was progressing in the novitiate. They expected to arrive sometime during the morning.

"Ah, God bless you, Brother Dominic—you're right, I'd forgotten completely. Um . . . how would it be—er—we have no other guests just now, no retreatants? Good. Well, how would it be if I come across to the guesthouse after Sext and eat with them at midday? We can talk as we eat, and that will leave me free this afternoon. If they eat in my house, I know what will happen; they'll relax and get expansive, and I shall have trouble getting rid of them in time to have all the account books and everything set out. Bless you; thank you so much for reminding me—please let me know if they don't appear during the morning. If they're delayed and arrive in the afternoon, they can eat with me in the evening in my house and stay over."

John retraced his steps to the day stairs and knocked at the door of the novitiate. Brother Felix answered it, which meant the door opened as silently as if a ghost had turned the handle, possibly quieter. Felix gave his novice master cause for concern. Theodore thought he seemed obsessively perfectionist and felt fairly sure that no man who needed to get everything right could last the course in monastic community—especially if his obsessions were allowed to progress to an interest in everybody else getting everything just right. It couldn't happen. Sooner or later chronic disappointment would escalate into conflict.

"Can I help you, Father Abbot?" Brother Felix spoke in such carefully hushed tones that John wondered if the novices were in deep meditation and to be under no circumstances interrupted, or if this novice had a sore throat.

"Can you send Brother Cassian down to see me?" John felt faintly exasperated with himself that whatever was bothering Brother Felix communicated powerfully, so that he found himself matching the novice's undertone.

"Certainly, Father. Is that all?"

"Yes, thank you." John felt foolish as the two of them murmured at each other with such coy and excessive discretion. As he turned away, his exasperation showed on his face, and Brother Felix, closing the door silently after him, wondered if he'd said something to offend. Their abbot didn't normally seem irritable. He trod meekly back to his seat, his eyes downcast, examining the exchange to think what he could possibly have done to improve his demeanor and conduct.

"Was that Father John," asked Theodore. "Yes? What did he want? Brother Cassian? Now? Yes? Off you go then, Brother—oh, it's because your parents are visiting, isn't it! Find out from Father Abbot when he will be seeing them, so I can fit in some time with them around that. Now then: the theology of the Eucharist—yes, my brothers, still! Are you all right, Brother Felix?"

Brother Cassian slipped out of the novitiate, glad to be free of a morning's theology, interested to be given some time alone with his abbot, whom he liked, excited at the prospect of a visit from his family. He hoped his little sister might be coming with them too, and his aunt.

Abbot John ascertained from him that though the long silences of monastic life had searched out demons he didn't know he had, Brother Cassian was enjoying his time in the novitiate. He liked the other novices (most of them), he loved Father Theodore, he enjoyed his work in the pottery with Brother Thaddeus and on the farm with Brother Stephen, and he felt proud and privileged to be part of the community at St. Alcuin's. John took him back to the demons of the silence and probed a little as to what those might be. Finding they were the usual terrors of loneliness and inadequacy, old buried sadness and personal vulnerability, he concluded that essentially he had here a healthy and basically capable, sane young man who should contribute stability and normality to the corporate personality of the brethren. He walked across with him to the guesthouse when word came that Cassian's family had arrived, with a feeling of relief that at least this seemed to be simple. He liked Brother Cassian's family. Forthright, good-natured, chatty, they were delighted to meet him—respectful but not overawed, and John felt comfortable with them. He dispensed Brother Cassian from attending Sext when the bell began to ring, excused himself, and left them to enjoy each other's company until lunchtime.

As he sat with them later, relishing Brother Conradus's cheesy herb bread and a bowl of tasty pottage with little pieces of meat from the pigeons they'd eaten yesterday added in, Abbot John felt tension he had not realized was there leaving his body. He could do this. For once something was pleasant, something was rewarding and cheerful and easy to accomplish; he savored the time with them and admitted to himself a profound reluctance to leave their company for the task of rescuing the finances of the abbey with Brother Ambrose and Fathers Chad and William.

Meanwhile between the guesthouse and the claustral buildings, in the abbey court, Father Chad came across to help Brother Ambrose and Father William carry to the abbot's house any ledgers that might be needed for their conference.

"Well, thank heaven somebody's come!" exclaimed the cellarer. "I've not so much as caught a glimpse of Father William since Chapter! He was not present at Sext so far as I could discern, nor has he even looked in here this entire morning. I must say I'd thought he'd be along here directly—to give some explanation of himself and make an apology—for this is a pretty mess and no mistake that he's created for us to sort out!"

He stared in indignation at the prior. "What do you make of it? I don't know, I'm sure! What kind of a man is he? I'd come to rely on him—I'm not getting any younger and he seemed so capable, seemed to have his hand right on everything that had to be done. And now look!"

Father Chad nodded thoughtfully. "What puzzles me is why he didn't ask anyone's permission. I don't know what he was thinking of, just to take matters into his own hands as if the place were his private mansion. It shows a level of disrespect and lack of submission that I find most disturbing—*most* disturbing!"

Weighed down with outrage and ledgers, the two of them walked from the checker to the abbot's house, where they found only Brother Tom.

"Come in," he said. "I'm sorry, I'm assuming Father John's still over at the guesthouse with Brother Cassian's family, and Father William's not here yet. But I've lit the fire for you, so make yourselves at home. Shall I take those books and put them out ready on the table?"

On this autumn afternoon, the daylight shone mellow, but the air was chilly, and the two men welcomed the sight of the fire. They sat in the two chairs that Brother Tom had set ready by the hearth, Father Chad leaning forward to spread his hands toward the warmth of the flames, Brother Ambrose sitting back with his feet on the hearth. Steam began to rise from his boots.

A quick, peremptory knock on the door that opened in from the cloister announced William's arrival.

"I'm sorry to keep you—where's Father John?"

He addressed these words to Brother Ambrose and Father Chad, with a brief nod of greeting to Brother Tom, who thought he saw courage protected by the armor of brusque concision.

Neither of the senior monks at the fireside turned to look at him as he brought the two stools that remained to sit on, placed them to make a group of four, and joined the other men as he seated himself on one of them.

"He is with visitors, we believe," Father Chad said eventually. Then he turned to look at William.

"Is that all you have to say? I'm surprised at you. I understand you have not been in the checker all this day. I should have thought you owe Brother Ambrose an apology, do you not, for this debacle? You should be ashamed of yourself! Father Abbot was merciful to you—remarkably merciful—in Chapter this morning. I would have expected a man to be scourged for such an offense as you have committed. It seems to me he let you off very lightly indeed. You ought not to take his leniency as a matter of course or conclude that what you have done is something of little moment. Have you nothing to say to me or to Brother Ambrose here? After acting behind our backs in the way you have, and now making yourself scarce all this morning once it's come to light?"

Brother Thomas, sitting on the scribe's stool at the far end of the room, could not see William's face but saw his body freeze as if he had been turned to stone. Some minutes elapsed in which William did not speak.

"Well?" Brother Ambrose joined in. "Have you nothing to say for yourself?"

William spoke then, softly, as soft as velvet, and for a moment his voice brought back with startling recall to Brother Tom the appalling stay he had endured with Father Peregrine in St. Dunstan's Priory. There was somehow something dangerous in William's tone, for all he spoke so very gently in reply.

"Yes," he said, "yes, my brothers, you have every right to question me. What have I to say for myself? Well, to you Father Ambrose, I think I have to say that if I had been the cellarer of this abbey, we should not have got from Lent to nigh on All Hallows with five hundred pounds gone adrift unnoticed; I'd not have been relying on another man to supply me with the information. I beg your pardon that I was not available for censure earlier in the day. I'd had enough. I hoped you might understand. And in response to your various questions, Father Chad, yes, I am most deeply and bitterly ashamed of myself. Not because what I have done has flouted your authority, for I feel no more respect for you than I would for a rabbit, but because what I intended as good work in gratitude for kindness shown me has grievously damaged and imperiled this house as things have turned out. I am not insensible. I am painfully aware of what I have done. I hoped I'd managed to communicate that this morning in Chapter, where you both were. And Father John—you are half-right: it is not that he was lenient as you thought, but that he was indeed—as you said—merciful. I fully expected myself that I would be scourged. But he knows that I . . . that there are . . . he knows me better than you do. And, thank God, he is not as absorbed with his own self-righteousness as you are."

"How *dare* you!" Quivering with indignation, his face crimson, hardly able to speak, Father Chad, who was not easily moved to anger, rose from his chair and stared at William in complete outrage. "How *dare* you suggest that Father John is self-righteous? After all he's done for you?"

What? thought Brother Thomas, bewildered. Then—when William replied in that same provocative, suave purr, "I didn't say Father John is self-righteous; I said you are"—Tom slipped from his seat, let himself quietly out of the room, and went with all speed to the guesthouse where he found his abbot making his farewells to Brother Cassian's family.

Brother Tom stood just within the doorway, saying nothing, but he looked very directly at his abbot, who surmised that all was not well and left his visitors at once.

"Father, I think you'd better come," Tom said quietly as his abbot joined him.

"Oh, my Lord!" was the only thing John had to say as Brother Tom apprised him of the exchange that had taken place in his absence. Walking with all speed across the abbey court, Tom felt slightly surprised to discover himself put to it to keep pace with his abbot's stride.

"What's going on?" demanded Abbot John with no preliminaries as he walked through the door that led in from the abbey court, followed by Brother Thomas who shut the door behind them and unobtrusively resumed his earlier seat.

William was on his feet the instant his superior entered the room, and Father Chad and then Brother Ambrose followed his example without delay.

"Sit down!" John instructed them, and they did. "Tell me what's happened! Brother Thomas has called me from our guests because of ugly antagonism here, and I would like your account of it, please."

"Father, would you prefer to take this chair?" Father Chad asked him meekly.

"No. I'm perfectly happy on a stool. Father William? Tell me, please."

Somewhere below conscious awareness William registered that the tic that had begun in his face in Chapter was still plaguing him and that he felt suddenly extraordinarily weary.

"It was me," he said, his voice flat and defeated. "I was asked for an apology for the disrespect I have shown and the damage I have caused to Brother Ambrose and Father Chad, reprimanded for my failure to come to the checker this day long, and my response was discourteous and inflamed indignation into anger. I ask your pardon, Father, and I am sorry to have encroached upon your conference with your guests."

He stopped. Brother Tom felt, as though it had been in his own body, the tremendous effort it took him to add, "And I ask your pardon, Brother Ambrose, and . . . and yours too, Father Chad, for my churlishness and extreme discourtesy. Please forgive me."

Neither Brother Ambrose nor Father Chad said anything in reply to this.

"Thank you." Brother Tom saw the gentleness with which John spoke to William hit him like a springy branch flicking back in his face. He reflected how odd it is that a man braced for pugnacity or blame will be completely undermined by kindness, and so it was now. William turned his head away, and Tom saw that his face had become a mass of tics and twitches. *Holy saints*, he thought, *this is starting to be too much for him*. He saw that their abbot had observed it, too. John drew the attention of the other men away from William.

"We have to pull together in this, my brothers," he said, his voice calm and reasonable (*infirmary voice*, thought Tom). "This spat between you three here is the querulous bickering of worried men, and we can't afford it. This is no time for blame now, for we have serious work before us. It is nobody's fault anymore. Father William was grievously out of order in what he did, but he knows it. Keep before your minds that though the result has been calamitous and his actions could not be condoned by any of us, his intentions were motivated by love for this community and gratitude, and surely we would want to treasure that.

"Besides all that, I am surprised to hear that you sought an apology from him. You had no business, either of you, to upbraid him in this way. You had your chance to have your say in Chapter this morning. Were you not there? Did you not see him? Was it not apparent to you how filled with shame he was, and how penitent? Have you not remembered that the offense was forgiven? It's done with. It's over. That's our Rule, our life, our faith, our gospel. The difficulties we are met to resolve will not disappear, but the sin is done away with. The problems we face now belong to all of us, but they are nobody's fault anymore. You are grown men, not children, and you are monks, servants of Christ who chose to accept the sin of us all. What are you doing, pointing the finger and recriminating and squabbling?"

His senior brethren accepted this rebuke with wooden faces. Tom thought they did not look entirely convinced. But they said nothing.

"Let's get to it then. You have brought the ledgers? Oh yes, your pardon, I see them on the table there. Let's take our chairs to the table and look at practical possibilities, work out the sums involved. Father William, I think we are relying on you for some guidance and suggestions."

As he said that, Tom's heart went out to William, who looked as though he could hardly carry his stool across to the table, let alone find his way out of a complex financial crisis. As he sat down to comply with John's request, a picture came unexpectedly into Tom's imagination of a worn cloth in the last stages of disintegration, left hanging out to dry long ago, rotted by fierce sunlight, blown by the wind onto snagging thorns, soaked by rain and stiffened by frost, forgotten.

William took a deep breath and reached for the ledger on the top of the pile. "It's not very difficult," he said quietly, "but it will take discipline and tenacity and mindful attention to detail—and those are the things it's ambitious to expect a community of this size to remember or sustain. One man on his own can be ruthless with himself to get where he means to be; it's not so easy to achieve the same result with a group."

Tom watched him. He looked almost dazed, and his hands shook. His face still twitched unremittingly. Tom listened with increasing respect and admiration as, despite this, William took them through every single aspect of the abbey's finances with a clear grasp of the exact extent of the capacity and potential of every area of work and resources both within the abbey buildings and in every further reach of the estate.

When he had done, Tom saw from their faces that the three men listening to him had taken in probably a scant half of what he'd said, but that they felt cautiously encouraged. They admitted a hope that he would be able to pull them through.

The afternoon office had been delegated to Father Theodore's capable hands. It was nearly time for Vespers when they stacked the account books again and stood to go.

"Shall I take them back to the checker?" William asked Ambrose, his voice humble and low. But Brother Ambrose said he thought he'd take them back himself, if Father Chad would help again. The prior readily agreed.

"Would you like to dine with me tonight?" John asked William quietly as the two senior monks departed with the ledgers. He meant it as a kindness, to protect William from the further society of his brothers on this difficult day, but William looked at him with something approaching incredulity. "I . . . Father . . . I mean, thank you—but of your charity, please will you excuse me? Can I—may I have your permission to go to my bed?"

His abbot instantly gave his permission.

Half an hour later, his handkerchief bundled against his mouth to keep his torment silent and private, William curled into a ball under his blankets in the austere, narrow haven of his cell and gave himself up to the convulsion of grief that had waited all day to have its way with him. He watched the carrion feeders of self-hatred and despair close in to tear his soul apart as he faced what he had become and what he had done. Every man entering monastic life renounced personal wealth and status, but there were other currencies than social standing and bags of gold. Trustworthiness and integrity; obedience, truth and humility; authentic chastity and simplicity—these were the treasures of monasticism. As William dodged and stumbled and lost his footing in the futile flight from obliteration, the ghouls that harried him overwhelmed him and began to devour his living spirit. He had been arrogant and deceitful and dishonest; he had disregarded his abbot's authority and flouted the principles of his obedience; he had thrown celibacy out of the window and traded simplicity for the twisty, winding ways of his own cunning. His integrity was shredded into filthy rotting tatters, and the light of Christ that had with such unexpected sweetness illumined his soul was nothing now but a broken lamp and a spreading stain of spilt oil on the floor of his darkness.

His last coherent thought was the dawning horror that word of the loss of the ship and the ruin it had brought would inevitably somehow reach Madeleine; there was discretion and kindness here, but there were never any secrets for long. He knew he must find a way to let her know himself. Groping for some kind of possibility, he thought he would go in the morning and tell Mother Cottingham what he had done. He imagined seeing the disappointment in him clear in her face, but thought he could cope with even that better than wondering every day if the news had reached them. After that his soul crashed completely. Talons of self-loathing ripped and lacerated his mind; paroxysms of sobbing twisted his belly into agony. He was lost; he had become devilish to himself.

"Oh Jesu, mercy . . . have mercy on me . . . oh Jesu *help* . . . " he moaned softly, pulling the handkerchief away from his mouth after an hour of this, so that at the very least he could pray.

"Have mercy on me . . . have mercy on me . . . " he whispered over and over, his soul crawling out of the filthy degradation it had slipped into, to the only sanctuary he could still find: the inexhaustible pity of Christ that turns no one away. He didn't know what happened to him then; his bankrupt, bleeding soul managed by some means to crawl out of what he had fallen into and beach itself on the shores of God's infinite love. He could do no more. Shuddering with the cold of complete prostration, he fell asleep there.

While William faced his personal demons in the solitude of his cell, Abbot John dined alone in his house, feeling the need for the solitude to frame his homily for the following morning, and glad to turn his thoughts to something other than accounts. He allowed the complexities of pressing concerns to recede from his mind, turning his attention to the preparation of his thoughts for his duties tomorrow. He had been thinking about the Eucharist all that summer and was still bringing its myriad aspects and insights before the faithful at Chapter Mass now in October. His novice master's request that he address the community on that subject had set him off along that train of thought, and he was still turning it over and over. The longer he gazed on the rich and intricate tissue of grace and redemption he saw there, the deeper and more beautiful it seemed to become in his eyes. He found himself falling in love with Christ in the Eucharist in a new and more profound way than he had experienced before, and this he hadn't expected. He had accepted the obedience of the abbacy as God's call on his life, but out of a sense of duty rather than any kind of enthusiasm. He found it humbling and daunting and hard. As his personal agonies of grief gradually settled and healed over, he had focused on learning the shape and rhythm of his work—and fielding the earth tremors that William sent his way, of which this last was surely the worst. So it took him by surprise to discover that in the midst of all of it he still heard the song of God's love, still experienced the wonder of the story of salvation as it unfolded in the everyday life of his community.

He found himself tracing the skein of resonance running from the telling of the Last Supper to connect with other moments and events in the New Testament. Alongside giving his mind to untangling St. Alcuin's financial dilemmas as he slowly chewed the raised pie and bean salad of his supper, he allowed his soul to expand into the glory of God's loving-kindness, the grace that reaches down and touches every living soul.

"I don't flatter myself for a moment that you stow away in your hearts every homily I offer you," he said to them at Mass the next morning, by which time the thoughts that had been developing had distilled into definite form. "But maybe you recall me speaking to you a while back about the Eucharist and how Christ's command, 'Remember me,' is obeyed in the living fabric of our lives in community.

"His words have stayed with me, 'Remember me . . . Remember me . . .' and then I came across them again in my own devotional reading in the Gospels, 'Remember me,' in a connection I had never made before.

"Jesus ripped the bread apart and poured out the blood-red wine in that last supper with his friends, and the grisly death he foretold caught up with him swiftly enough. Mocked and tortured, nailed by his hands and feet to the cross, he was raised up and left to sweat out his agony in the blistering heat of the sun. Crowned with thorns, blood trickling down into his eyes, a notice tacked above his head, *Jesus of Nazareth King of the Jews*, Pilate's strange acknowledgment of what had happened. Either side of him, two thieves endured the same execution, in punishment for what they had done. Punishment in their case deserved—inasmuch as anyone deserves punishment more than understanding, or a human being can do anything that deserves being nailed to a cross.

"And the Gospel story relates that one of the thieves mocked and jeered at Jesus. Personally, I'm staggered he found the strength or motivation—I think under those conditions my thoughts would have been occupied with myself. Anyway, apparently that's what he did, but the other thief took issue with him and defended Jesus against the unjust raillery. 'The good thief,' we've come to call that second man. We don't know what he'd appropriated that wasn't his to handle, whether it was only trifling things or amounted to a great deal; we only know he'd taken something he shouldn't have, and now he was paying the price. The good thief. It's very pleasing to me that we hold those two words together—there's always more to a man than the things he's done wrong. I like it, 'The good thief.'

"It's what the good thief said that I've been turning over and over in my mind: 'Jesus, remember me when you come into your kingdom.'

"The same words, d' you see? 'Remember me.'

"The cross as an instrument of torture pulls you apart. You hang on your arms. They dislocate unless you shift your weight to your nailed feet. The soul of a young man is not ready to leave his body. It takes something severe to tear the living soul out of a strong young man—he does not die easily. This really was a dismembering; the man was being torn apart—his soul ripped out of his body, his body dragged apart as his strength ebbed away. And he asked Jesus, 'Remember me when you come into your kingdom.'

"Jesus promised him, of course, that he would that very day be with him in paradise. He did what the man's community seems to have been incapable of doing—he forgave him.

He healed him of his sin and its consequences, laid it to rest, finished with it, stopped its power right where it was, so that it could not follow him and make a hell of his eternity.

"So the story holds out to us a hope that even if this life tears a man apart, dismembers him, the power and grace of Christ will re-member him, make him whole, heal him entirely, on the other side of the grave. That's a wonderful hope. It feeds our brothers in the infirmary here as they gradually relinquish their strength and ability to the decline of illness or old age. As they feel their vitality ebbing away, they lay hold on the good hope they have in Christ, knowing that once the labor of dying, like the labor of being born, is over, they will have all things in the One who has gone ahead of them, redeemed them, won them by the steadiness and the sacrifice of his love.

"But as I pondered this and turned it over and over in my thoughts, looking at it, looking into it, I found myself thinking, Wait on! There's something more here for us in this story; this is not just about the final healing of death. It's about another kind of healing that finds us right here.

"The good thief said, 'Remember me when you come into your kingdom.' That says to me that wherever and whenever Christ comes into his kingdom, we can confidently expect people will be healed. They will be remembered. What they have lost will be restored—innocence maybe, or humility, or generosity, or faith, or hope; men lose those things along the way. They don't mean to, but life hurts them, events are too much for them, and before they know it, sourness and cynicism, aridity and unbelief have grown over the eyes of the soul like the cataracts that cloud the eyes of an old man. And the things that came apart, that they looked down in horror and saw dismembered, will be made whole again—a sense of vocation maybe, or their good intentions, or wholesome discipline and faithful practice of their calling. Those things unravel easily enough, and we discover, dismayed, that we cannot put them together;

we have nothing in us that can glue what is all unstuck and good for nothing anymore. We need making whole again. We need re-membering. And where Jesus comes into his kingdom, that can begin.

"So—where *does* Jesus come into his kingdom then? When I asked myself that, I saw that we don't have to wait until we die. We don't have to watch the atrophy and withering of what we might have been, as the harder realities of life obtain their hold on us and knock out of us the hope and innocence we once had. We can start now.

"Jesus comes into his kingdom wherever and whenever a human heart says he can—it's as simple as that. We can't *finish* the kingdom in what we choose and build and practice here—but we can surely *begin* it.

"Wherever we choose to be honest with each other and allow our vulnerability to be seen, wherever we choose to be gentle when we could have been exacting, wherever we choose to forgive when we could have borne a grudge—the kingdom of Jesus grows, his reign extends, hope and life are raised up in us, and the grip of all that sours and diminishes us is weakened.

"It is as we are faithful, as we are gentle, as we are humble and kind, that we remember the human and open the way for the kingdom of Jesus. So I—or you—can be the good thief in our fragile and faltering humanity, begging him: 'I am lost, I am broken, I am done for. Please put me back together again. Please heal me. Forgive me. Please remember me.' And in so doing we also open the way for the kingdom to begin."

As always, when he had finished speaking John folded his hands into his sleeves, closed his eyes, and allowed his brothers to sit for a while with what he had said to them. He found this a difficult discipline, as though he attached weight to his words when he thought really they were not worth much of anyone's attention. But Father Theodore had said he must do this, must give the brethren space to stay with the teaching he had brought them—and he remembered that this had been Father Peregrine's practice always—so he did it, too.

The monks sat in choir in the order of their arrival into the community. So it was that Father William occupied the stall at the end of the row of solemnly professed brothers on his side of the chapel. Father Theodore, as novice master, sat immediately opposite him with the novices sitting in the stalls below William's and Theodore's.

Loving what John had said to them, Theodore sat in quiet contemplation, his chin resting on his hand, exploring the spiritual territory his abbot had left them in. The novices for the most part sat in exemplary reflection, eyes closed, hands folded into their sleeves, some thinking, some feeling hungry, some daydreaming, some just waiting for the sound of the community rising for the *Credo*. Brother Robert, sitting directly next to Father Theodore, knew that this proximity diminished his novice master's capacity for surveillance, too near to know if Robert's eyes were open or shut or what expression he had on his face. Provided Robert did not fidget enough to attract his novice master's attention, there was freedom in his location in the chapel. Sometimes he looked up at the rich blues and rubies of the stained glass in the great east window. Sometimes he scanned the faces of the monks who sat across the chapel from him, wondering about them—not his brothers in the novitiate whom he felt he knew all too well by this time, but the fully professed brethren in their remote existence. Today he was watching Father William's face (as he often did, sitting almost opposite him) with idle curiosity.

William would close his eyes in this time of silence after the homily. On this morning Robert watched with increasing fascination as he noticed the beams of light, subdivided by glazing bars in the windows, reflecting on a steady trickle of tears rolling down William's face. Tears were commonplace in the novitiate, as were infectious tides of laughter. Father Theodore told them it was because of fasting sometimes, and from sleep always disturbed for the night office. Only occasionally, he assured them, did the easily triggered weeping arise from personal difficulties or challenges to the spirit. Brother Robert wondered if this remained true for the fully professed brothers. He thought they would surely have come to terms with the life by the time they took their solemn vows—reached a substantial equilibrium in their inner walk. What was wrong with this man then? There was only so much that filtered through to the novices, so much they conjectured (with or without adequate basis for any informed conclusions), and that left so much they simply did not know.

It happened again. This quite often happened. As he watched Father William, intrigued and interested, suddenly he found himself looking into William's unsettling eyes.

Robert, never a sensitive man, had not the wit to see that those eyes full of despair and brimming over with tears were saying to him, "Please . . . please don't watch me . . . please don't look at me . . . "

William bent his head so that his cowl shadowed his face, affording a degree of privacy. Even then, Brother Robert could see the tears still fell, and William simply let them fall. Robert wondered if his nose was running, too. He couldn't see but he thought it must be. Personally, when he cried he felt urgently the need to blow his nose. He thought it must take an unusual level of indifference or restraint to sit unmoving and just allow the tears to fall. He wondered which it was. And then he heard the knock of Abbot John's ring against the wood of the abbot's stall, and the community rose as one to join in the *Credo*. As the brothers turned to face the high altar, Brother Robert caught out of the corner of his eye a momentary, discreet flash of William's linen handkerchief.

At the end of Mass, the novices reverenced the presence of Christ in the reserve Sacrament behind and above the altar, then waited their turn and followed the professed brothers out of the choir—more in file than procession, for though they followed their order precisely, it was done with no pomp or ceremony; the monks handled the holy routines of prayer as unaffectedly as a housewife carded wool and set it up on the spindle. Brother Robert stole a curious glance again at Father William as he left his stall. Pale and distant, that face bore no visible trace of emotion anymore. He just looked very, very tired.

CHAPTER
FIVE
November

*I*t was needful to light a candle in the checker now when work commenced again after the office of None. Between Vespers and Compline only the moon and the stars lit the velvet sky. Abbot John made his way with care across the abbey court this November night, for it was very hard to see anything at all. Inside the little building, William automatically reached up his hand to shield the candle flame as he heard the latch click; the day had been blustery, and the draft from the door would blow out the light.

"Brother, what are you doing here?"

John closed the door behind him, and William let his hand drop to the table again.

"You should not be working at this hour—especially not on concerns like these. You need a fresh mind for accounts. And it's too cold in here."

William looked up at him. The kindness in John's face twisted like a knife in his belly, unbearable. Sometimes, just because he loved him, he wanted to tell him everything, tell him he had no vocation now if he ever had one at all, tell him he wanted Madeleine more than anything and that love suffered and festered in his viscera, wearing him away day after day, like a shackled prisoner covered with sores hidden out of sight in the darkness of the dungeon under the house. He wanted to tell him it didn't matter how late he worked or what occupied his time; it was all the same.

"I'm all but done," he said. "The last of the Michaelmas rents are in, and Ambrose has left the chits out for me to enter the details. Not everything tallies—as usual—and if I have to chase up any underpayments and pleas of hard times, it has a better chance of success if I do it sooner and don't wait until they've relaxed in the delusion that I won't have noticed, spending all their money meanwhile on more attractive options than paying rent. There'll be monies to find for grain; I was sick at heart to see so much lying smashed down in the fields when we had those sudden rainstorms early on. It still comes before my mind's eye when I think about it. And I was mortified that we hadn't the spices to embalm Oswald. His family would have preferred to be present when we buried him. Still, on the bright side, when I explained why we buried him so quickly, they sent a handsome gift—which was generous because he refused to send any kind of word to them to let them know where he was; didn't want them to see him mutilated. I wrote and told them all that had happened, and I think they were a bit shocked that they'd thought he'd died but he'd been alive all this time. But they only found out he was alive from me writing to say he was dead. They were grateful, though, that we'd taken care of him. I'll show you the letter. Sorry, I should have brought it to you before; it just slipped my mind. So anyway, some money in from them, thank the Lord. Oh—and the lace—I got back the price of the lace, amazingly."

His abbot listened to all this, taking in what was being said to him, and quietly watching and assessing while he listened.

"Are you quite well?" he asked when William finished speaking. William blinked in surprise. "Why? Am I not making sense?"

"Perfect sense. But you're worn to a wraith. There was

never that much of you, but you're a bundle of bones now. Your face looks hard and drawn and lined—kind of desperate. You've aged. You have a grim, dusty look about you; the whole light about you is gray. Your eyes are red, and that's the only color left in you."

"Try the soles of my feet," responded William, "you'll find they're a lurid shade of yellow. But I'm pleased to hear I am so easy on the eye."

Even as he offered this banter in reply, he could feel his belly tightening in panic. What if by some unimaginable miracle he found a way to offer himself to Madeleine, and she saw a haggard old man at her door for whom she felt nothing but pity?

"You were never easy on the eye." John took up his jest. "But you haven't always looked as frankly terrifying as you do now. Are you eating properly, William? Are you sleeping well? I expect the truth, mind!"

William groped for some quip to turn aside the unwelcome exposure these questions threatened, but he could think of none. He shook his head. "Not really," he muttered.

John frowned, and William felt extremely uncomfortable under the thoughtful probing of his gaze. At least John's putting a distance between himself and William had kept William safe from the perspicacity of those kind, brown eyes. William wished they were not considering him so very carefully now.

"Is it that you are troubled about the money, or is it still Madeleine—or both?"

William averted his face, his lips compressing into a tight line. He didn't want this conversation.

"I see," said his abbot. "Both, then. Is there anything you should be telling me?"

Then William met his gaze, and despair flashed like anger in his face. "I am doing my best, all right? I am doing my best with everything! I pray and I work and I struggle! I'm trying as hard as I can, and it may not be good enough, but what more can I do?"

"Eat," said John, "and rest. I'll ask Michael to sort out some herbs to help you. No—don't just dismiss it like that. You will break your health permanently if you go much further down this path. You eat your supper and take your ease by the fire in the warming room in the evening, and I'll ask Michael for some doses that will send you to sleep at night. And if you will not cooperate with this, shall I tell you what I will do? I'll have you out of here for a month in the infirmary and leave the accounts to Brother Ambrose, and I'll give you into the special charge of Brother Conradus to be fattened up. You think I'm jesting, don't you? Well, I'm not. Leave this now. It's an account, not a boiling pot of stew or a sheep with an obstructed labor. It won't have altered between now and tomorrow morning. I will sit down here and wait just while you pack that lot away, and then I want you out of here. And you're coming across with me to the infirmary for some sleep herbs."

William continued to look at him.

"The warming room?" he said. "Did you mean that?"

"I did. Is that—that's a comfortable, friendly place to be—is that difficult?"

He saw the horror around William's mouth. "You would rather avoid the warming room?" John asked. "Is it haunted?"

It was a clumsy, feeble jest and found no answering gleam of humor.

"I cannot bear the idea," William answered him simply. "I never go in there—well, only occasionally to check the fire irons and make sure the benches and tables have no worm and all the joints are good."

"You don't like the idea of relaxing with your brothers in community?"

"*Relaxing?* God in heaven! I am here on sufferance, John! I was despised when I came, I have caused nothing but trouble,

I have all but destroyed the whole future of the common life—oh, face it my brother—they do not love me."

It was a confession not lightly made. John looked at the worn-out face and hollow eyes that regarded him with such tired resignation. He knew he had to bring some healing here, but he had to tread carefully. William would detect any half-truths and prevarication with effortless ease.

"I don't see," he said finally, "how anybody could really know you and not love you. Part of building your future in this community is allowing the brothers to get to know you. That's all it would take for them to love you."

William felt the welcome touch of kindness on the soreness of his soul. But John's words also brought home to him that he did not want to build his future in this community. He had to be here, that was true. But the thought of consciously shaping and working for a future that severed him from Madeleine and cauterized the wound of separation opened a dizzying glimpse into a holocaust of despair.

Puzzled, John watched the parade of ghosts and shadows that crossed his friend's face. He wanted to reassure him, release him from the obligation he had laid on him. But instead he said, "Not every evening. But three times a week anyway. You have allowed yourself to be too much alone. This is a community, my brother, and you are part of it."

William nodded, and the look of misery intensified. "I know," he said.

"Well, come now; you should not still be working at this hour—I want to set you up with some medicine in the infirmary before we go into silence. These things will still be here in the morning."

John wished he had brought a lantern as they went out into the blowing dark. A fitful rain fell in a fine wind-flung spume, and the damp night felt raw and discouraging. William hunched his thin shoulders against the dismal weather as he felt for the keyhole, inserted the big iron key, and locked the door of the checker. He had given up returning the key to Brother Ambrose—he always got there before him and worked until Compline every night, obsessively examining accounts and calculating possibilities.

The wind flapped and snatched at their habits as they crossed the court and dived into the cloister buildings for a moment's relief from the wildness of the night before they came out on the other side and made their way to the infirmary. The path from the cloister to the infirmary John could have walked with his eyes shut. William lagged behind him a little. It was of no use trying to follow a man in a black habit on a dark night; the path was familiar enough to him too, but he was glad of the glimmers of moonlight on puddles and stones.

"Brother Michael," said their abbot when they found him in the dispensary preparing sleeping doses and draughts for coughs and pain, "I have brought you this man because he is exhausted. I think I'll leave him here with you for a couple of nights."

John turned as William started to protest. "Brother, are you arguing with me? You have had pneumonia once this year; I am not risking your health over a pot of money. I will not have it said that any man succumbed to exhaustion and nervous debility on my watch. Two nights only. In the daytime tomorrow you can do your work as usual, but just until supper time. After Vespers you come back here and do the same as tonight, which will be to take a cup of hot milk and honey with sleep herbs infused in it, and take your rest until Chapter. And you will take your midday meal here in the infirmary—yes, you *will*. What's the matter? Why are you shaking your head at me like that?"

"Father, I . . . I have to pull us out of the hole I've got us into. I have to be clearheaded, and I have to have the evenings to work on the books—the daytime is so taken up with attending to people and checking things and going hither and thither after different men's needs and concerns. And besides . . . "

"Well?"

"I have no right to be calling on the resources here. The infirmary was short for herbs and spices before the consignment I ordered went to the bottom of the sea. I can't come here and be using up such candles and precious medicines as we have—'Brother, I'm in pain, I can't sleep, can I have something to help me?' 'No, Father William's consumed what he hasn't lost.'"

The bell for Compline began to toll. "Leave him here with me," intervened Brother Michael, who had listened to William and watched him thoughtfully as he spoke. "Perhaps you will help me, Brother, take these doses to the men who need them, and then you and I can take a hot drink together and talk about this. Come, my brother. It's a while since I've had a chance to spend time with you; I've missed your company."

Abbot John smiled as William reluctantly acquiesced. Brother Michael put into William's hands a tray of physic doses to carry and laid a couple of cloths over his arm, and John withdrew without another word, giving silent thanks to the God who had made and molded Brother Michael from the dust of the earth and then set him walking in the direction of St. Alcuin's infirmary. *One less thing to worry about tonight*, he thought as he hurried back through the gusting rain to the candlelit choir, there to settle the day, the world, and the community down to rest.

William offered no small challenge to any man charged with managing him, but Brother Michael proved equal to the task. Before the brothers in the chapel had sung the last responsory, William found himself tucked into bed with a hot stone at his cold feet, his belly less tense than it usually felt, comfortably warmed by a hot, sweet, milky drink, and an unfamiliar feeling of peace pervading his senses as valerian, oat, hops, and lavender did their good work. His last thought before he fell asleep was that he couldn't quite account for how this had happened to him because he couldn't remember agreeing to it exactly at any given point.

The next day he found he could concentrate better than he had been, and when he ate with Brother Michael in the infirmary instead of taking his meal in the frater with the community, for the first time in a while he was able to eat without feeling sick. He made no further protest against his second night in the infirmary, but the day after that filled gradually with dread as he contemplated entering the warming room after Vespers in the evening. He was not entirely sure he could force himself to do it, but it had been required of him as an obedience, so he tidied away his work at the end of the afternoon. He still had the key to the checker. He might have been told to limit his time there, but he would not have it further limited by what Brother Ambrose might choose to do.

When supper was over and Vespers had ended, William sat in his stall, shivering in the coldness generated by damp stone. Eventually he went out into the cloister and, refusing to allow his mind to dwell upon it just as in childhood he had refused to allow his mind to dwell upon what might or might not await him when he came home, he pushed open the door of the warming room and made as unobtrusive an entrance as he could.

He stood just within the door. Most of the community seemed to be gathered here, enjoying the fire on the great stone hearth this dismal November night.

Brother Bernard and Brother Giles sat with their backs to him at a table not a yard into the room. Opposite them sat Brother Walafrid, a pewter mug of ale in his hand, nodding in agreement as Brother Bernard elaborated on what were evidently strong feelings about a subject he'd been developing before William entered the room.

" . . . after all, it's not as though there was ever anything wrong with the way old Ambrose did things—he left us in peace and he got things done eventually; he did what was asked of him, and at least he never managed to bring us to the brink of complete ruin."

Brother Walafrid glanced up and kicked Brother Bernard hard when his eye fell on William standing there. But William didn't care. He agreed with Brother Bernard. It was what he expected, and this was why he had dreaded coming. He'd overheard worse of himself on plenty of occasions before. He walked quietly past the table without looking at the monks who sat there. A hand tugged at his sleeve, and he became aware of Brother Thomas, sitting with Brother Cormac, Brother James, and Brother Theodore. "Come and have a mug of ale—Brother Cormac brought a couple of jugs over that were left from supper. Move over, Theodore, he's not that skinny!"

"No, I'll not take a mug of ale," replied William in response to Brother Tom's repeated invitation as he sat down gratefully in the company of these four men, in whose eyes he read only friendliness.

"Why not? Go on—you need stoking up a bit! God help you, you're as thin as a lathe! There's some nuts here too—help yourself."

Brother Thomas watched in amusement, shaking his head at such unbelievable self-denial as William took two nuts and poured himself barely a nipperkin of ale, but he said nothing. As William set the jug down with quiet care, Cormac picked it up and, without looking at William or asking permission, added more ale to the mug until it was half-filled. "Take it," he said. "You've earned it. You work hard enough." How did Cormac know, wondered William, what the cause of his reticence had been? But Brother Cormac did not try to catch his eye and said no more to him. "How's Brother Robert?" he said instead to Theodore. "He was scrubbing the day stairs when I brought up that string you asked for this morning—looked mighty sorry

155

for himself. Another half hour and I think it would have killed him."

Theodore smiled. "He's a good lad, and he doesn't object to rolling his sleeves up, but I think scrubbing floors was always women's work in Brother Robert's family. It came as a bit of a shock to discover who would be doing it here. Mind you, I've spared him the spectacle of Brother James sewing button-holes—I think that's cap-strings and petticoat country to him."

Tom laughed. "Aye, it's a different world once you take the women away! You certainly discover the rags and brooms don't do it by themselves. Have another nut, William—just one, mind, you don't want to overdo it."

William felt the understated kindness of these men fold around him. He could not imagine how he could ever express his gratitude at the restraint of the tactful gentleness with which they included him. The hour he had steeled himself to endure passed more quickly than he'd anticipated.

When the sand in the glass ran through, Brother Peter got up and left to start the bell ringing for Compline. Tom went to the fireplace where he kicked and prodded the burnt remainder of logs into place amid a shower of sparks to make all safe to leave. Father Chad crossed the room as the bell began to sound, pausing to say to William, "It's good to see you here, Father. I can't think you've spent an evening with us here at all that I remember. The fire is very welcome now the nights are getting chill, don't you think?"

As he looked up at the prior from the bench where he sat, William felt guilty that he had carried with him his scorn and resentment toward Father Chad. He appreciated this gesture of friendship. "The fire is welcome indeed," he replied. The prior smiled at him and said "It's been good to have your company," and joined the other men making their way out of the door for chapel.

"Do they ever bother to clear away their beer mugs? Pigs

might fly!" observed Brother Cormac as he rose with the rest of them. "Well, I'm not doing it now; it can wait until morning."

"Do you have your head above water?" asked Theodore quietly, coming alongside William as they made their way to the door. "Just? Well, I have prayed for you—and for all those who are dear to you." William looked at him, startled. He knew him to be Madeleine's confessor, but he couldn't believe she would have actually told him any of what had passed between them—would she? Theodore's face held only kindness and gave him no further clues. Theo stood aside to allow William to precede him through the door, and they followed the other men along the cloister and into the choir.

"*In manus tuas, Domine, commendo spiritum meum.*" Brother Gilbert's voice left the beautiful melody of the versicle on the damp November air.

"*In manus tuas, Domine, commendo spiritum meum,*" came back the echo of the brothers' response.

"*Redemisti nos, Domine, Deus veritatis,*" the cantor continued.

As the community sang the response, "*Commendo spiritum meum,*" William suddenly had the feeling someone was looking at him and glanced up in the direction of the parish altar. There, on the threshold of the choir, hesitant and not wanting to interrupt them, but clearly agitated, stood Madeleine. William murmured an apology to the novices in the stalls below him as he slipped past them to see what was amiss. The disturbance was very slight but attracted the abbot's attention. He saw William go light and swift to where Madeleine stood and gently put a hand to her elbow to guide her out of anyone's earshot to tell him her trouble.

"It is Mother Cottingham," she whispered. "William, I am so sorry to intrude like this, but there is no one in the guesthouse or the porter's lodge, and she begged me to ask for you. She is—William, I think she is coming near her end."

"Wait for me," he said. Madeleine marveled, as she often did, that the brothers had this trick of speaking so muted—not a whisper, for that is sibilant and can carry, advertising what is said, but an undertone that barely breathes on the air and yet is heard. "It's all right," he added. "I am with you." He gave her elbow a little squeeze, and she felt instantly comforted.

He trod briskly and quietly along to the sacristy, fetching a fair linen cloth, a bottle of holy water, the little pot of chrism, and the key for the tabernacle in the Lady Chapel, from where, briefly bending his knee in reverence, he retrieved the blessed Sacrament for the Viaticum.

"Have you a crucifix in the house?" he asked Madeleine in the same hushed undertone, and she nodded.

The blessing was said, and the brothers were finishing the *Salve Regina* when John appeared at their side, his face questioning.

"Mistress Cottingham is passing; she has asked me to come to her." William betrayed no sign of impatience as he waited for his abbot to give permission, but Madeleine's eyes fixed anxiously on her brother's face. He nodded. "Go," he gave his consent, and the two of them went with all speed through the small door in the narthex, hurrying along to the abbey close as fast as they could, given that they could hardly see anything in the dark and now lashing rain.

William paused for a moment as he followed Madeleine into Ellen's cottage. The fire was built up compactly on the hearth, warming the air, which herbs scented with a clean and wholesome aroma. He saw that the floor had been swept and strewed with rosemary, that all was neat and well cared for, the pots scoured and set orderly on the dresser. Nosegays of herbs hung in bunches from the rafters, and their fragrance had mingled with the woodsmoke until the house smelled as beautiful as incense.

"Come quick!" she insisted, and he followed her up the

stairs, ducking to avoid the low lintel as he came up into the bedroom. Here again all was calm and well tended. Mother Cottingham lay tucked in her bed under several blankets—soft, good-grade wool, William noticed. Her hair had been brushed for her and spread loose on the pillow. In addition to the lovely fragrance that permeated throughout the warm, dry cottage, William caught the scent of lavender here and detected the source of it in a small willow basket stacked with bunches of the dried flowers on the floor near the head of the bed. He took in that Madeleine had lavished every resource she had on this old soul, as well as her time and loving care.

"You have done well here, my love," he said quietly. Mother Cottingham opened her eyes. When she saw William, her fever-flushed face wrinkled into a smile. "You came," she said.

Her words were faint and hard to discern. William recognized the problem from his own bout of pneumonia; she had neither the breath nor the strength for speech. Even that short phrase left her panting, and her words formed in her mouth only, backed by no power from her chest or diaphragm. The bellows of her lungs were blocked solid.

He returned her smile and turned to the small table Madeleine had cleared of everything but a crucifix and a dry sprig of hyssop she had left in readiness. He could feel the feathers of death's angel brushing close to this house, and he set about what he had come to do with dispatch.

When the sacred vessels and elements were laid out on the little table, he gave his full attention to the woman in the bed, drawing up the low, three-legged stool that stood by. He took her hand. As he looked at her, they heard the door latch and the sudden rush of gusting wind downstairs, then footsteps mounting the wooden stair to join them. Abbot John, ducking his head as William had, came quietly into the room. He said nothing but glanced round for somewhere to sit, and Madeleine lifted a shawl and towel and bowl from a handsome carved chair in the corner by the window. William turned his head to look at his abbot, his eyebrows raised in inquiry.

"Go ahead," said John quietly. "I did not come to take over or intrude."

"God bless you, mother," William addressed himself to Ellen as he held and stroked her hand. Madeleine sat down on the old footstool next to John in the carved chair. "Do you mind these two being here?" Ellen shook her head, turning her face toward him, her trust and love shining clear in spite of the extremity of her condition.

"Have you anything to confess, my dear?" he asked her gently.

"Nay . . . " The weightless rasp of her voice hardly stirred the air. "I am done . . . with all of that . . . now . . . " She stopped, closing her eyes, her breathing distressed and quick. A light sheen of sweat began to gleam on her brow. "Only . . . my son . . . I was angry . . . with thy abbot . . . on account of thee . . . " She stopped again, gasping uselessly for air. "And it was unjust . . . of me . . . I ask God's pardon . . . "

Panting, perspiring, weak, she gave herself to the effort of breathing and said no more. William waited lest there be more, and then he said, "That's all? Yes? Then know that you are forgiven, absolved by Christ's death on the cross for you of every earthly sin. I will anoint you now, dear heart, if you are ready." Eyes closed still, she gave a little nod in assent.

He gently withdrew his hands from hers, took his holy water and the sprig of hyssop, and sprinkled the water on her in the shape of a cross. "*Asperges me, Domine . . . *"

The fragrance of chrism blended with the perfumed air as he anointed her and spoke the beautiful words of blessing and forgiveness. He placed a fragment of the host upon her tongue, the soul's strength to begin this most momentous journey home, and he absolved her of every weight of earthly sin, so that nothing might hold her back or impede her way. " . . . *Per Christum Dominum nostrum. Amen.*" And it was done.

Mother Cottingham opened her eyes and watched William as he covered the holy things on the table with the cloth he had brought and came back to the stool to sit beside her again. She gazed on his face as if she was fixing it in her mind forever, and her features moved in a smile through which tenderness radiated like actual light.

"My Will . . . " she whispered. "Oh, tha'st been . . . God's gift . . . of a son to me . . . My Will . . . my Will . . . never fret . . . my child . . . all shall be well . . . "

Then with an odd, bubbling exhalation, the labored gasping ceased, the shining love in her eyes vanished as suddenly as a candle blown out; all that was left was an aged body in a bed and the fragrance of lavender, woodsmoke, chrism, and healing herbs. In the silence the wind sounded loud again. "Go forth upon your journey in peace," William murmured. He reached forward and drew down her eyelids over the staring eyes and held them shut firmly so they would stay that way. Then several minutes passed in which they did not speak or move as the moments suspended and they tasted eternity, feeling death's angel gather up God's child and take her home.

Eventually William got up from where he sat at the bedside. Madeleine watched the bleak, pale, neutral mask of his face and noticed the tendons of his neck and his habit belted around almost nothing as he gathered up the things he had brought from the table. He did not look at her. He could not, she knew, while his abbot sat quietly observing, his chaperone. She wished John had not come. She wished she could comfort William; she could see the ragged wound of loss this death had left.

"Are you at peace about the last offices?" her brother asked her, and she nodded. "Yes. Yes, I would like to do that for her."

"Has she near kin?" he asked next.

"She has not," William answered him. "Nobody in the world."

"Then we can lay her to rest as soon as Brother Thomas has dug the grave," his abbot said. "I will send Brother Michael with a winding sheet, Madeleine, in the morning. Is all well with you, sister? You are not afraid to be left here with her? Is it—are you all right to be left alone?"

Madeleine smiled, a small, tight smile that made John feel obscurely unwelcome, as though he had irritated her somehow. "I have done this many times before, my brother, and often alone. I am not uneasy nor afraid of death. What I wanted was this anointing for her before she passed. With that done, all is well. What she needed is fulfilled."

John nodded. "Come then, Brother. I'm glad we were in time."

William stood holding the things, his face reserved and set. He did not reply nor did he look at Madeleine. His abbot stood back to allow him to go first down the stairs, and William did not even risk a glance in her direction as he passed her.

She stayed where she was. The staircase creaked slightly under their tread. As they reached the room below, John called up, "I'll leave the fire to go out, yes?" And she spoke in affirmation.

She heard the latch lifted. She heard John say pleasantly to William, "She loved you more than I had realized. You must have become like a son to her, from the way she spoke your name."

The latch clicked again, and she did not hear William's reply. She sat down on the stool at the bedside and reached down to the basket of herbs, taking a bunch of lavender and tucking it into the limp, dead hand of her friend. Madeleine had been many years familiar with death, and this passing brought no tears. Even so, she would have given more than she could express to feel William's arms close around her in comfort in this moment. She stayed there only a few minutes. She wanted to wash Ellen's body and lay her out before the corpse began to stiffen. She went downstairs to warm some water on the fire.

As they reached the abbey, going in through the abbot's house where Tom had set a lantern burning against his abbot's return, John paused and looked at William.

"Do you know," he asked as he closed the door behind them, "why Ellen Cottingham was angry with me—on your account, she said?"

William paused before replying. He had hoped John hadn't heard that said. He had no wish to add to the lies that already separated him from his friend. He looked up at John, and his eyes flickered though his tone remained neutral.

"She didn't say, did she?" he said. "Father, I must take these things back to the chapel before I go to my bed—if I have your permission?"

John considered this. He could feel that both Madeleine and William had firmly shut him out. Uneasy, he weighed up whether there would be any point in pursuing it further and decided he would probably make things worse. It would be better to trust them.

"Oh—yes, by all means take those bits," he said. "If you can see, that is. It must be getting late by now."

He opened the door to the cloister, and William went quietly on his way. *Have I lost him?* John prayed silently as he held the lantern and watched him gradually disappear into the shadows between the moonbeams. *Have I lost one of the sheep you gave into my care?*

Madeleine, in Ellen's cottage, went about her tasks with patient care. She washed the old woman's body and laid her out, weighting her eyelids and twining her feet in place, plugging every orifice, dressing her for burial, brushing her hair and composing her hands. She covered her with the top sheet of her bed, folding and setting aside the blankets. She snuffed out the candles but left the fire to die out by itself; soon enough the room under the roof would become cold, and she thought it as well to keep the cottage dry—it would not stay warm for very long.

She took the key from the hook and wrapped her cloak around her, locking up the cottage and returning to her own home next door. She had made up the fire before she left to see to her neighbor, and the downstairs room still felt comfortingly cozy.

She pushed off her clogs and took off her cloak, hanging it up on the nail near the chimney beam, where the warmth of the embers would air it, and took the key for safekeeping to the box she had for important documents and valuable possessions. As she lifted the lid, she remembered that it actually had something in it. All her own valuables, and the one precious letter she had treasured from her father, had been lost with the cottage at Motherwell; this box had remained empty for several weeks. But at the beginning of October, Mother Cottingham had given her a letter addressed to Abbot John. "This must not be given to him yet," she had insisted, "he must not even know of it. But when I die, tha must put it into his hands with no delay."

Madeleine touched it, wondering what it said. She laid the key to Mother Cottingham's house upon it and closed up the box until the morning. Then she bolted the door to her house, used the poker to drag out the hot stone from the ashes, wrapped it in the linen towel she had ready, and took it upstairs to warm her bed. Fitfully, as the clouds scudded across the face of the moon, enough light came into the cottage that she could manage without a candle. She took off her dress and stood in her shift and woolen stockings, considering changing into her nightgown. It felt forbiddingly cold to her touch. So she took the soft shawl that William had procured for her when she left the Poor Clares and wrapped it around her, burrowing under the blankets. She curled around the cloth-wrapped stone that she kept near her belly as a talisman of comfort and hope and friendliness. Her feet stayed warm enough with her stockings still on.

She lay awake for some time, unmoving, aware of the moonlight through the window, the different influences of warmth and chill around her body. She saw again, vivid in her mind's eye, William bending, gentle, over Mother Cottingham, the evidence of the bond of love that had grown between them so clear. She relived the washing and laying out of her friend. The smell of aromatic herbs that filled her own cottage recalled the fragrance she had achieved in the house next door, subduing any contagion, bringing peace and serenity to the hour of death. And like a series of portraits she saw William's face . . . William coming swift to discover her need in the chapel . . . William listening intently to her trouble . . . William casting an appraising eye over the cottage as he came in through the door—and evidently approving . . . William, his expression serious and reverent, absolving her friend, by the power vested in him as a priest, from all earthly sin . . . William, his eyes lowered, his face set, disciplining himself not to look her way as he left the house. And he looked very thin, she thought, and not very well. She worried about that for a few minutes, but weariness overcame her then; it was late, the moon well advanced on her journey across the night sky, and Madeleine drifted off to sleep.

When the morning came, though she rose with first light to milk her goat and let the hens out of their little wooden house, she heard the Mass bell ringing almost before she had them fed and the goat tethered out on the border of greensward within the abbey walls. This privilege felt uncomfortable at times. It had struck other inhabitants of the close as a good idea, and they had petitioned the cellarer for permission to do the same.

"No." William's response had been unequivocal.

"But Mistress Hazell has a goat out there."

"She does. But you may not."

"'Why can we not have goats there if Mistress Hazell does?"

"Because it is not within the terms of your corrody."

They invariably argued, and always to no avail.

"No, no, and no. You are wasting your time on this, and mine. It is not permitted. Mistress Hazell's situation is not the same as yours. She has one goat, she will never be allowed more than two at the most, and it is out of the question that goats should proliferate within the abbey walls. Absolutely not."

"That man's as hard as nails!" they muttered, but they bore neither Madeleine nor the abbey any ill will, only William. Madeleine was good to them and seemed to have a solution for every ailment; the abbey was a just and responsible landlord. But William, they agreed, had a heart as soft and yielding as black granite.

Madeleine couldn't help smiling over this as she hurried to Mass, having ducked back into her cottage to snatch up the letter to give to John. It seemed so incongruous to juxtapose the face William turned to the world with the vulnerable, tender man who had stood in the darkness of her cottage and poured out his love.

She slipped into a place near the back, for they were reading the epistle already when she came into church.

After Mass she walked round to the abbot's lodge, where Brother Tom answered her knock at the door.

"Wes hal, Madeleine—I'm sorry to hear of Mother Cottingham. Father said her passing was peaceful, and you had cared for her as if she'd been a queen. I've to dig the grave for her this morning—in our burial ground, Father Abbot says, for we were her family really, and she never went to church anywhere else. He'll be in very shortly if you care to wait here out of the cold—he's only struggling out of his vestments; he'll be along in just a moment."

He had hardly finished speaking and she had barely entered the room when John came through the cloister door, and she gave him the letter. He broke the seal, asking her, "Is all well? You are not too cast down after yesterday? Oh—this is telling me I must inform her lawyer and giving me the address. Joseph Haydon. It means someone will have to go to York and let him know. She says we can find him in a yard off Goodramgate. Brother Ambrose or Father William, I suppose. Or Father Chad. He might do it. Did you know Mother Cottingham could read and write, Madeleine? There was more about her than I realized, I think. Thank you, sister—I'll take this to the checker, and we can act on it at once."

They went together, he to the checker and she beyond to the close. The grave would be ready by the afternoon, he said. They could bury Ellen after Mass the day following. He had spoken to Brother Michael after Chapter, and a winding sheet would be made ready and brought across to her during the afternoon. Someone would bring the bier round tomorrow, in the course of the morning. John wanted to know if she thought Ellen had died of old age alone—there had been no sign of plague or any contagion that might give cause for alarm? She reassured him, no; only the natural course of things had had their way. All was well.

Then as their ways parted, John stopped and looked her in the eye. "Sister, I hope you don't feel I've been too harsh about you and William. It would never be my wish to hurt you."

Madeleine hesitated. She had never expressed anything to her brother of her love and the hardship of separation. William had no opportunity to tell her of what he might have communicated to John. She was fearful lest this prove a trap—not that her brother would make it intentionally so, but she must be cautious in reply.

"William?" she said. "De Bulmer? How might you have been harsh?"

She knew her brother well; he did not take kindly to being deceived. He spoke evenly in reply, but she could tell he was displeased with her. "Yes, *de Bulmer*. Good day, sister. Brother

Michael will come with that cloth for you later on. It'll take Brother Thomas most of today to dig the grave. We can bury her tomorrow."

✠   ✠   ✠

They laid Mother Cottingham's earthly remains to rest under a graceful beech tree, a little apart from the brothers' graves in the burial ground. The night rain had cleared away, and the day turned out mild, except it was windy up there on the hill. Brother Ambrose and Father William attended her burial, and Brother Thomas who would stay behind to fill in the grave again. Brother Martin had come up from the porter's lodge—Brother Richard had promised to watch the gate for him. Father Chad would have come, but he had set off directly after Chapter to York, taking word of her decease to Mother Cottingham's lawyer. It occurred to Madeleine that Father Oswald would have stood beside her today, for he had spent time in her cottage often and had got to know Ellen better than most while he was there. His grave, still mounded and bare of grass, lay only a few yards away, near the lichened drystone wall that bounded the graveyard.

The abbot spoke the words of blessing, reciting the psalm and the *Pater Noster* and committing her soul to God as they lowered her into the earth. Observing from a discreet distance as Abbot John said the burial prayers, Madeleine watched William's face, very pale against the black of his cowl. He shed no tears for this old woman; his expression remained impassive, but then neither did Madeleine weep—it was a timely and natural death. Even so, something in her felt profoundly sad. She would have given much to ask him what his heart held and what the still mask of his face hid, and what the friendship had been between himself and this ancient widow that brought such a radiance of love to her face in the hour of her passing as she bade him farewell.

Then the rite came to an end, and after a natural interval of silence, the brothers turned away from the grave. Brother Thomas waved to Madeleine and went to fetch his shovel from behind the tree.

Brother Martin and Brother Ambrose started down the hill together, their boots and the hems of their habits already sodden from the wet grass of the track.

John and William came across to where Madeleine stood. "Are you bearing up?" asked John kindly, and she nodded. Evidently he had forgiven her prevarication of yesterday.

She looked at William then, and as he met her gaze, she saw a whole sky in his eyes—not the harmless blue and white of this day, but his own sky: storm clouds and drizzling rain. What kind of man, she wondered, carries his own sky in his eyes?

"It's been a year for burials," he commented, his voice empty of emotion. "First your mother, then Oswald, now this."

John, beside him, lifted a hand to his shoulder and held it there, comforting. "Yes. A great deal of sadness. Still, we clawed you back twice from the edge, my brother."

"You did," replied William quietly, "and for what?"

John squeezed and patted his shoulder. "Nay, don't say that." He cast about for something to add, along the lines of *You've been a blessing to us* or *We wouldn't be without you*. But William knew well enough with what affection he was and was not regarded, and John knew it would ring false. The community understood its duty to a man, and would stand by him, but the privations of loss of income were beginning to bite. William was not popular.

"To be what Mother Cottingham said, maybe?" Madeleine said into the silence. "'God's gift of a son'? Your friendship laid a salve for her on many years of pain. It was not a little thing."

William's face twisted, and she saw then that he was hurting through and through.

"Everywhere I look, there is nothing but things dead and lost and broken and . . . "

He shook his head and lifted his arm up across his chest, gently closed his hand round John's to remove it from his shoulder, and walked away from them, setting off back down the track.

"Skin and bone is that man," remarked Madeleine. "What's the matter with him?"

John looked at her, disconcerted. "Do you truly not know?"

"I think I'm asking you what you know," she replied.

"I know he has lost his peace because he has walked in ways he was not called to," John answered her.

She turned her face to let the wind blow her words away as she said, "Yes. But which way do you mean?" And she started down the hill. John followed her. He could see there would be no gain in pursuing this conversation. He had never expected the abbacy would make his life easy, but this was not the kind of impossible knot of difficulty he had been imagining.

"Madeleine—my sister," he said as they reached the bottom of the track and the ground broadened out. "Please—I beg of you—don't seek a quarrel with me. There is only so much I can do, and I don't see how . . . it's . . . I am caring for him the best ways I know. That's all I can say. What would you have me do? Give him into your care?"

Like the clash of two wooden Saxon shields in battle, their eyes met.

"'Tis I could heal him," she answered softly.

For a moment John looked down at the ground. "I am choosing not to hear that," he replied then. "You are here as this abbey's guest, and I am its abbot. It is my misfortune and my obedience. Before I am your brother, I am the abbot here. Before I am his friend, I am his abbot. I have to choose and decide in faithfulness to that. You will have to be content with knowing that with things as they are, you might not have been suffered to stay on. You have your welcome still, but tread carefully, for it cannot weather everything. 'Tis Christ can heal him; there is no other herb of grace to touch the heart's true core."

She nodded. "I can't gainsay that. Well—God give you good day, Abbot John. But I have to say—the contentment I am finding is as good as the peace I can see in you and the healing I can see in him. There should be a better way. There really should. Nay, it's all right. You were seeking my confidence, I think; well, there, you've had a little of it, and it only made you chide me. I know my part. I shall not disgrace you."

Help me, John murmured under his breath as he stood still and watched her walk away. *Help me. Help all three of us. Find us a solution, my good Lord. I can stand firm, but this is driving pain in deep. Look into our hearts, of thy mercy, and help us find a way out of this quicksand we seem to have stumbled into. For Christ's sake. Please.*

The day did not improve. Brother Stephen looked glum at the midday meal, and inquiry discovered they had a cow with mastitis, and a fox had taken one of the geese in broad daylight. Brother Thomas seemed preoccupied with his thumb at None, and when John asked to look at it afterward, the swollen sullen purple alarmed him.

"You've got something in there. Go straight to Brother Michael for some drawing ointment and get it bandaged. I'm sorry—I'd not have let you handle graveyard dirt if I'd known you had that. No—it is *not* nothing, and I'll warrant it's hurting bad."

When the bell rang for Compline and the day came down to night, John was glad to see the back of it. He prayed desperately that tomorrow would bring something better and that they could find some upward path out of this dreary sequence of disasters.

Through the next morning he prepared a talk for the novices about different kinds of prayer, as Theodore had asked him to do. John thought the young men would hardly be delighted to find that instead of a siesta, they had to come straight back from the frater to hear their abbot blundering through the steep places of a landscape he felt ashamed to pretend he knew. He recognized it must be done and picked up the texts he'd brought from the library to show them, when someone knocked at the door from the abbey court. He hesitated and decided he at least had the time to tell them to go away. Brother Martin stood on the step, wanting to tell him that Father Chad had returned, bringing the lawyer from York with him, and should they come straight over?

"No—that is—er . . . no." John hesitated, but decided the novitiate had priority since the visitor would need in any case to stay overnight. "Refresh the man and make him welcome. I won't be all that long. I'll send word to the guesthouse as soon as I'm free. Ask Brother Ambrose to keep him company to give Father Chad a bit of a break."

When the lawyer heard that the abbot was busy, he looked irritated. He had to make two calls in the village before his return to York.

"I have to see a woman named Madeleine Hazell as well," he said. "She dwells in the cottage adjacent to Mistress Cottingham's, I understand? I know my way there. No, I need no sustenance, thank you. We stopped on the way."

He walked briskly along the abbey close and found Madeleine at home, checking her supplies of herbs and tinctures for winter colds, much depleted by her care in recent weeks of her ailing neighbor.

She invited him in and offered him the comfort of her fireside, amused by his desiccated manner and the prim composure of his face. He looked, she thought, like a man who would regard human emotion as a pointless self-indulgence. He asked to sit at the table instead, where he unrolled and set out the deed and scripts and records he had brought her. She listened intently to what he had to tell her, accepted the documents as he handed each one into her keeping, and then made him go through it all again. Even then, she found it hard to take it in. She asked him a number of questions and was just satisfying herself that she had assimilated the news he had brought her when another knock came at her door: Brother Ambrose this time, telling her visitor that Father Abbot had returned to his house and would see him now.

Thomas Haydon got up from her table. "You understand all, Mistress Hazell? Those were the terms. My instructions were to impart this to you alone. You comprehend what I have told you? Write to me if you have any trouble, or I will be here until the morning, should you need more clarification. And you are alone? You have no husband? No son? No father? This is important."

"There is only my brother," Madeleine replied. "I have no other family."

The lawyer waved this aside. "Your brother does not count. He is a monk. He cannot own property. Well then, good day!"

He dipped his head in a quick bow and turned to Brother Ambrose. "We must go via the guesthouse," he said. "The documents I need for your abbot are all over there."

Madeleine stood in the doorway watching them go. She saw them enter the guesthouse, then emerge again shortly after and walk across the court to the abbot's house. She waited until she had seen them admitted and satisfied herself the door was closing behind them. Then she set off along the close as fast as she could go, without drawing the attention of anyone who might notice her by breaking into a run.

She arrived breathless at the door of the checker and glanced back, thanking God with all her heart that nobody was on their way here and William, rising to his feet in surprise as he saw her in the doorway, was alone.

She went in and turned to close the door but changed her mind. It would be immodest indeed to be alone here with one of the brothers.

"Listen!" she said. "No! Listen! Don't touch me, don't kiss me, don't speak to me—just *listen*! I don't know how much time we have, and you must take this in."

He had come forward to greet her, but perched on the edge of the table. "Go on then," he said.

Hardly reaching her conscious mind, an arrow of gratitude whizzed through Madeleine's soul that she had found a man who could take a woman seriously enough not to bluster when she told him (imperiously) what to do.

"'Tis Ellen's will. She has left me riches. There is a house and eight pounds a year settled on me, but she has also left me a second sum in trust. From that sum I may take the interest only, until I marry, when it passes to my husband as an annuity. If I never marry, I can have the interest of it until I die, and then the capital sum goes here to the abbey. Do you see? Do you see what she's done? William, she has set us free! She has given us a house and an income, a way clear to be together!"

Breathless, excited, she stopped and tried to calm her breathing. William had his hand at his mouth, rubbing his chin thoughtfully as he considered what this meant.

"When will you go?" he asked. She saw with surprise that he weighed this news cautiously. The sunburst of eagerness and delight she had expected did not come.

"I don't know—straightaway—I don't know—what shall we do?"

"The thing is . . . " He hesitated, and she saw the struggle in his face. "I don't know if you have heard about this, because I told Mother Cottingham but I've not seen you to tell you, but I made a huge, huge blunder in the spring—with the money—

and I have brought this house to the edge of complete downfall. I think I can turn things round again, but I'm certain no one else can. I don't really see how I can leave them now. In another year, possibly—not certainly, possibly. But not now."

She stared at him in dismay. "You mean—she has done this, given us a hope and a future, and you *won't come*? Do you not—have you misgivings—have I mistaken you?"

He shook his head slowly no, and she saw the hardship of it in his eyes, leaden now and drained of every joy. "You have not mistaken me. I have no misgivings. But I have been the worst kind of fool, and I just have to stay here until I've put it right. Will you . . . can I ask you . . . will you go ahead and wait for me, if I come as soon as I can?"

Madeline felt the amazement of hope and freedom starting to bleed away. Unbearable this, to have so near within her grasp the love she had yearned for, only to find it must be deferred by months and months and months.

"Oh you complete . . . dolt!" she exclaimed, glaring at him in absolute frustration.

He nodded. "Indeed. You have it right. That's what I am."

Then as approaching footsteps sounded on the gravel of the abbey court, he slipped back onto the stool behind his desk, and she found herself looking down onto an upraised face saying to her with pleasant expression and neutral tone, "No, there is no question of it at all. Two goats at most, Father Abbot said, and yours only. It is entirely unfair that they should have sent you thus to speak on their behalf. It is a fruitless inquiry, and they already know the answer to their request. It is the same as when they asked me back in October. I have—oh, good day, Brother Ambrose, that took very little time."

"Trouble about that goat of yours?" Ambrose smiled kindly at Madeleine. "Well, I'm sorry to interrupt, but can it wait? This man from York insists he has to have you present, Father

William, before he will go through with Father John what he needs to say. I can't think why."

"I'll be getting along," Madeleine said as she stepped back toward the doorway.

"Madeleine—I will do what I can. I will do my best."

Brother Ambrose's cheery laugh split the air and made them both jump. "That's a promise to beware of, Mistress Hazell! This brother's best is sometimes more than meets the eye!"

Seeing his joke found no favor whatsoever with William and raised only a distracted smile from Mistress Hazell, Brother Ambrose felt embarrassed and guilty. Perhaps he had been unkind.

"Well, anon—they will be waiting," he said more soberly, and they went to the abbot's house while Madeleine returned to her cottage, with nothing to hurry for now.

"Ah! Here he is! Good. Bring a stool to the table here, Father William," said his abbot.

Down in the village at Motherwell, when John was a boy, there had been a man who was viciously cruel to his dog. He kept it for ratting. It had been kicked and sworn at, beaten and starved, until it lost the will for anything at all. Dull of eye and cowed in manner, it no longer cared about life. It was past biting or begging; it no longer chased interesting smells; it just lay outside its master's hovel in the cold with its face turned away from the world and toward the wall, completely defeated.

Watching William's face as he pulled the stool across to the table brought that beaten, broken animal back with a sharp, unexpected suddenness to John's mind. *Lord have mercy!* he thought *Whatever's happened to him now?*

"That's right; then I can begin." The lawyer's fussy, precise tones called their attention. William sat down on his stool and looked as interested as if he had been summoned to watch the fire going out.

"This is a most unusual will, most unusual. I have special instructions, and I have had to speak to the beneficiaries separately. In the letter she left with me, Mistress Ellen Cottingham was particular to ensure that the contents that relate to St. Alcuin's Abbey were divulged in the presence of its abbot and of Father William de Bulmer. Can you confirm, Father, that you are indeed he?"

"Aye, that's me," said William. John was relieved to see he looked at least puzzled now, not just desolate and bored.

"Thank you. Then here are the bequests Mistress Ellen Cottingham has made. She has three properties in the city of York that return a tidy sum in rent each year—I have the particulars with me, all the relevant accounts. One is a butcher's shop in Low Petergate, one is a leatherworker's shop in Spurriergate, and one is a merchant's home in a yard behind Stonegate. They are all trade premises with dwellings over. She has also a farm about halfway between here and York—a good-sized, thriving farm, a little east of Malton. Mainly sheep. Good income. Each of these properties, and the income related to them, she has bequeathed to St. Alcuin's Abbey.

"Then she has some money on deposit which she has bequeathed to the abbey—being the sum of four hundred and eighty pounds, fifteen shillings, and sevenpence, and the use and disposal of this is at the abbot's absolute discretion. There is also a second sum, however, a greater amount. She has bequeathed separately, but also to St. Alcuin's Abbey, a sum of five hundred pounds. This is to be used at the discretion not of the abbot but of the cellarer, in payment of any outstanding debts and for the purchase of provisions for the workshops and the kitchens and the infirmary, wherever it will be of practical use for the well-being of the community. This second sum, she bade me make especially clear, is given to the abbey with particular thanks to Father William de Bulmer for his gentle care of her soul. There are no conditions upon this sum; its connection with Father William is none other than that it is an expression of thanks for his care of her. He has no personal claim or call upon it. It is to supply the daily wants of the community here."

As Thomas Haydon stopped speaking, utter, stunned silence reigned.

"Have you any questions for me, Fathers?" the lawyer inquired. "No? I shall act for the estate in making the deeds of transfer to the abbey's ownership, and my fee is to be subtracted from the first of the two sums. Under any circumstance, Mistress Cottingham insisted, the five hundred pounds bequeathed in association with Father William de Bulmer is to pass to the abbey untouched by any other consideration or cost. I shall carry out all that is necessary, and I think you will see it is straightforward. If the lands and properties lie too far from here for you to consider practical to administer, I can (if you wish) arrange for their sale and see to it that you receive the monies realized in outcome of the transactions."

"Thank you." John recollected himself. "Thank you, indeed. I think we were just speechless, friend—I mean, who knew? She lived so simple and plain. Anyway, God bless her. Yes, we may well have questions later. I know you have business down in the village while you are here today, but perhaps you will care to dine with me here?"

Abbot John rose then to accompany Mother Cottingham's lawyer to the door, and Brother Ambrose went with him to the stables to see that all was ready for his visit to his other clients down in the village. William ignored their departure completely. John came back and sat down opposite him.

William sat gazing, thinking, gazing. "Oh I see . . . " he said softly at last. "'My will . . . all shall be well.' *That's* what she meant."

He seemed to snap back into a more normal state of being then, and he looked down at the documents spread on the table.

"I can take these and look at them, perhaps? Will you accept my advice on whether to keep or sell the farm? Not decide today maybe—ask Brother Stephen's advice and Brother Tom's. The shops in York—my first instinct is to keep them, but we can see how we go, surely? If I take these with me now, I can have something coherent for you at suppertime—that's if you want my company here, Father; forgive my presuming."

"Oh, yes indeed, I would be grateful if you join us, and for your advice which is always shrewd. Yes, take them—do. And you? Does this make some things better?"

William rolled the plans and scripts and deeds into one large scroll and looked up at his abbot.

"Better? I feel as though the whole fallen world has been resting on my shoulders and crushing me to death, and it's just rolled away. She has made everything better—not some things—everything."

John wondered how that could be and if perhaps William had been haunted mostly by anxiety about the money. Perhaps the thing with Madeleine was fading from his mind, even if not from hers. He sincerely hoped so. He held the door open for William and thought how fragile he was beginning to look. Even this good news, stunning as it was, brought profound shock, and in that moment William seemed as brittle and unstable as a lattice of ice. "Look them over, but don't work too hard, my brother," he said to him as he walked through the door.

"I'll tell you what you need to know by suppertime," William replied.

He took the documents to the checker and put them down on his table. Brother Ambrose had returned and was full of excitement at this new turn of events. But William, half listening, murmured an excuse. He left the checker and walked swiftly down the close to Peartree Cottage, and he couldn't care less who saw him.

Madeleine recognized the quick decisive knock. He had not intended going in, but he saw from her face she had been crying. He slipped inside the house, pushing the door to, and took her in his arms.

"It's all right," he said. "It's all going to be all right."

The frustration of brief explanations was something they both had to live with. They hastily agreed that Madeleine would go to the cottage that had been given them, and William would follow as soon as he had guided John through the abbey's end of the necessary administration. He thought it best that she go without telling John of their intentions. "Let me weather that storm once you are away from here, dearest," he said, for he privately thought the storm when it broke might be very bad.

"Can I ask you though," he said soberly then, "are you sure you really want this complete dolt to have and to hold? You will be a woman of property now and could have your choice of men. Do you truly want the real man I am? Some women . . . well, there are women who fall for the fantasy, and once out of the habit and the mystique of the monastery, the man himself, so ordinary, loses attraction. I haven't the skills of a householder. Away from here I am going to seem inadequate by anybody's standards. Are you sure, quite sure, my sweet, that you want me—the real me?"

"I'm not one of those women," she answered him, "and yes—I am quite sure that I want the real you."

CHAPTER
SIX

December

J ohn—" he whispered—"John, please let me go."

"*Let you go?* What d'you mean, let you go? Are you out of your mind? Do you think for an instant I'd be letting you *stay*, after this? You've betrayed me—deceived all of us! How long has this been going on? How long have you been hatching this? What kind of a deal did you strike with old Mother Cottingham? Whatever have you and Madeleine been up to in that old woman's cottage? How could you do this to us? Do you not remember how you begged us to take you in? And all this while you have been taking what we have to offer and presuming on our good fellowship while you plotted in this safe place some other private scheme of your own! How could you do it? Oh, you disgust me! I would never have believed this of you!"

There followed more of the same. William stood silently while this tempest raged round his bowed head. Eventually John stopped, biting off his last words abruptly. He glared at William, shaking with fury. "Yes—you can most certainly go!" he said coldly, quietly then. "How have you used us? What were we? Your inn, or your place of business? I never imagined it coming to the day when I would take the lash to any man's back, but by heaven, you would have felt it if I'd had any inkling of this."

William nodded. "And I should have deserved it. You can do it now if you like."

"To what end? William, do you not understand monastic life *at all*? Our scourge is not for punishment; it's for correction. It's for those who are struggling to walk in the way, not those who want to leave when the going turns uphill. It's for the monks—and as far as I can see, you are no monk, you're just a man in someone else's habit."

"Please, John. Can I speak to you? Will you listen to me? Can we sit down and talk?"

He raised his face to look at his abbot. "Please."

With a rough, vague gesture, John indicated the chairs beside the hearthstone. "Sit then," he said.

With evident reluctance, the abbot sat in the other chair, and so they faced one another. "I'm listening."

William swallowed. "It hasn't been quite as it looks, but I haven't behaved well either—and I'm sorry. I went to see her one night in the summer, and—"

"You did *what?*" John gripped the arms of his chair.

"Oh, peace!" William lifted his hands, palms toward John. "Brother, peace! Let me tell you. Please. Just—shut up!"

John was not breathing like a man at peace, but he let him speak.

"You are thinking we spent the night in her bed; well, we did not. I held her. I kissed her. I stayed there an hour. I was just desperate, John; I was going out of my mind with it. I thought if we had that one hour, I could bear it—lay it to rest."

"If you thought that, you must be more of an idiot than you look! *How* long have you been a monk? Do you think someone who'd been a postulant only a fortnight couldn't have told you better than that?"

William nodded. "Of course, they could. Of course, I was fooling myself, telling myself what I wanted to believe. Even before I left her house that night I realized what I'd done. If it makes you feel any better to know it, oh God, I've suffered for it. If I thought I longed for her before, that was nothing to how I felt after that hour. Anyway, Mother Cottingham saw me leave the close. She asked me about it. So I told her. I begged her to keep silence for us because I knew you'd turn us out if it was known. And bless her—she did keep our secret. Since that night, I kissed Madeleine again once; only once. And I took her in my arms, for she'd been weeping, one time in these last weeks. And that's all, John, and I'm truly sorry, for I did deceive you. At least—that's all we physically did, but for sure we went on loving one another. I tried to stop, I tried to renounce it, but I couldn't do it, I just couldn't. I could only pray to find a way for us to be together. But there was no arrangement with Mother Cottingham. I had told her about the money I lost, but this will came as a complete surprise to us. She believed in our love. She wanted it to have its day. And when I asked you to let me go, I was not for one moment entertaining the notion you'd let either of us stay here once this was known. My brother—please—are you listening to me?"

John's eyes looked like two black holes glaring back at him, hostile and full of contempt.

"Go on."

"When I first came to this place, there was so much anger, and all of it deserved, all of my own making. I've made hatred in the world by the way I've behaved. But I knew if I could find my way to Columba's house, I would find a shelter in Christ's mercy; he would hold his cloak over me."

"Who? Peregrine or Christ?"

William looked at him. "Yes," he said softly. "Exactly. I've worn Columba's cloak, and I have been sheltered, and was it the Master or the man? Both, I think. You made a way in for me, and you have been so good to me. I've never had a vocation. I've told you that before. Though the monastic way suited me well enough, I used it to my own advantage. But you—all of you: Michael, Tom, Conradus, Theodore, James, you yourself—you've stood up for me and spread your kindness over me. I shall never forget, never. I came here full of fear and cynicism, and I'd hardly been in the place a few days when I realized I'd come to learn how to love. I found myself kneeling to kiss Tom's feet and begging him to teach me how to love. And it hasn't been an easy lesson—by heaven it has not! I've thought it was going to kill me at times, the growing inside me of love. Clothed in Columba's habit day by day, that is what I've learned and what's happened to me. By inches, Christ opened me up. And then there was Madeleine, and now I am wide open. I have no defenses anymore. I love her so much, John, I really do. I love her so much.

"And I've come to understand that when you love someone, you don't bind them to you; you set them free. The loving itself sets them free. If we are possessive or selfish or unkind or full of hate, we build prisons. We bind the people we hate to ourselves with cords like twisted metal; they gnaw into us so we can *never* get them free of us. I hated Columba, and he worked into me like a painful splinter. I couldn't shake him off no matter what. But now I've learned to love him, and he has released me, not only from what I did but from all the horrible consequences of it. It's over. I'm forgiven. I'm free.

"I hope when you've had time to take all this in, and a few months have gone by, you might countenance the idea of being friends again. I hope you'll come and visit us in our home. I hope if you run into difficulties with the accounts and everything, you'll come and ask for my help—and if you do, my help will be so gladly and gratefully given, for I owe my life to you. But—I hardly dare say this to you—in the meantime I need you to truly let me go. And by that I mean I need you to let me go with understanding and kindness and humility, and then I will be free. If you stay angry with me, you will bind me with guilt and the resentment that goes with it so that I cannot be free of you, or you of me, even if you throw me out. And I am done with anger and hate. I want no part in it anymore. I came here to learn to love, and I have learned my lesson. Please let me go. Please let me go to where love is leading me. John . . . please."

John rubbed his forehead, tired and confused and upset as his rage subsided. "I don't know what to say," he responded eventually, avoiding William's eyes. "You betrayed me," he muttered.

William leaned forward in his chair. "I'm honestly sorry, John. Please forgive me. I haven't handled this whole thing well. Please understand—I'm not making excuses. I did try to keep faith with you. There were those two times when I kissed her, but, oh Lord, the nights I've lain awake in despair, the days I've trudged through not knowing how I would make it from one minute to the next—trying to be faithful because you deserved that. But now there is a chance for this love, that's ached and festered inside me in raw agony, to come true in my life. Please let me go. Please don't curse it and blight it and bind me to you here with hate and anger."

And as he listened to him, John saw what he meant. He sat in silence a little while longer, then said, though he still couldn't bring himself to look at William, "You can find yourself some clothes in the almonry store. You can take some money—enough to tide you over until you make your own arrangements, whatever you need. I cannot dispense you from your vows—you know that—because you are solemnly professed. Nobody can dispense you; it is between you and God. All you can do is marry Madeleine in defiance of your vows—and then they are in suspension unless, for example if you are widowed, you seek pardon and reinstatement. There is no clean way of doing this; you just have to go. If you keep your head down and do not advertise your identity and manage to live without attracting the attention of the ecclesiastical courts, you may hope to be not important enough to make yourself worth excommunicating. Shave your head completely so you will not advertise your history with your tonsure. Grow a beard. Be who you choose to be, and answer questions as you wish. The cellarer's work has introduced you to a wide range of people. You cannot hope to be unrecognized. But you can live quietly, without attracting more notice than is necessary—at least, I think you can, though what I've seen of you so far makes me not entirely confident of that. Go in peace then. Yes, you do have my blessing, both of you. If all of Christ's way is a way of love, perhaps you have a vocation after all. Maybe you've been looking in the wrong place for the last thirty years."

William relaxed, gratitude and relief shining from his face. John still wouldn't meet his eyes.

In the years he had presided over St. Dunstan's as its prior, William had often enough been in the place in which John now stood, as a man's vocation ran dry and he asked to leave. He knew the territory well enough. No good-byes, no latitude given, no time. He would be expected to leave now, since that's what he had asked for and got, without speaking to any of the brothers, no explanations, no farewells. It was a shameful thing. He went in disgrace. To turn aside from a vow made to God is a sacrilege. Such a course could never be condoned. William clung gratefully to John's willingness to say he gave the two of them his blessing, for he stepped out of every tradition of the Church in so doing.

The two men rose from their chairs. "John, will you . . . will you give me the kiss of peace?" William asked him humbly.

John stood quite still for a moment, and William felt his struggle, the turmoil of mixed emotions that had grown out of this parting tumbling and knotting like a nest of adders. Then without speaking, John stepped forward and embraced him, hugged him tight, with the desperate courage of a man who must press an iron spike into the vulnerable tissue of his heart. "Peace be with you," he whispered, "my brother, my friend. And

I didn't mean what I said about taking the lash to your back. I'm sorry I said it. Others have been there before me. You've been beaten enough for one lifetime."

As he felt the gentleness of William's embrace, even in that difficult, painful moment, John knew that in the course of this last year he had witnessed a miracle. He dimly grasped that if he could see this through with compassion, conduct himself with the understanding and grace of Christ instead of the stern coldness of ecclesiastical authority or the hot indignation of a man who has been deceived, he had the chance to allow the miracle to be made complete.

He kissed him—one cheek, then the other cheek—and releasing him, he looked into his eyes and saw the love and gratitude that he knew would be what he remembered in the end, and he could not be angry anymore.

"I'll come with you to the checker to get you some money," he said. "It might be better if it's me signs it out of the book."

Together they left the abbot's house by the door leading into the abbey court, and they walked across to the checker. Brother Conradus, returning from the guesthouse to the kitchen, saw them and waved cheerfully.

"May I speak to him? He's always been so good to me, and I haven't always treated him with the appreciation he deserves."

"No, you may not," John replied. "You should have thought of that before. That's the point of being nice to people. You never know when you won't get another chance. And you've made your decision; now you're going to have to live with it. You can't say good-bye to anyone, and you know that full well."

William said nothing. He did know, but the full impact of that knowledge had not made itself felt until he saw Conradus and had to pass him by. They walked on. When they reached the checker, William halted a few feet from the door. "Please don't make me go in," he said unsteadily, and John then saw the tears on his face and realized how much this wrenching apart was costing him. "I don't think I can face Ambrose. Please can I stay outside?"

John hesitated. "All right, wait for me here," he said, thinking it would in any case save awkward questions from Brother Ambrose, and went by himself into the building. William waited for him, leaning against the rough stone of the checker wall, tears cold on his face in the wind and bleak, pale sunshine of this December day, accepting the reality of what it meant to leave the abbey. He felt empty and sick and cold. He had been a monk since he was nineteen years old. Suddenly the thought of leaving the security of the Rule and the rhythms of life, the safety and strength of a community, seemed terrifying. He had no idea what kind of a husband he would make, no idea if this dream would deliver the joy and fulfillment the fantasy promised. He had never been a householder. He didn't know if he would still be vulnerable to the violence of rough justice outside the monastery. He knew he loved John, and he found the distance that must be put between them unbearable. *Will this never end?* he asked himself. *People being angry with me and telling me I'm no good . . . people hating me and despising me . . . contempt . . . getting everything wrong . . . being afraid and full of shame . . . will there never come a day when it's different?* In a miserable attempt to pull himself together, he felt for his handkerchief and rubbed the tears away, but they kept on coming.

As he waited for John, he reflected on the generosity with which the community had eventually enfolded him, and he felt bitterly ashamed to be turning his back on that. He could see that a man who wants to be accepted and included has to stay in one place, that the Benedictine vow of stability was the cornerstone of the monastic vision. But then, there was Madeleine. *A merchant went in search of fine pearls*, the Gospel said, *and when one day he found a pearl of great price, he gave everything he had to possess it*. William could identify with that. His whole life had been about shrewd assessment and cool evaluation, as a merchant's is. And then, like the desert blooming under a rare fall of rain, his heart had woken up; he had found what he was looking for, and he wanted Madeleine enough to give up everything else. But what if the dream went sour?

John came out of the checker with a bag of money. He looked at William and hesitated. "For mercy's sake, look at you! I think you and I need to go somewhere a bit more private than this before you're ready to walk out of the gate," he said.

"Thank you," said William wretchedly, his voice shaky. "Yes, please."

John sighed, a little impatiently. "Oh, come on; you'd better come back to my house until you can get a grip on yourself. Just look at you!"

So they trudged back the way they had come, and John opened the door of the lodge and silently stood aside for William to go in.

"Sit down," said John. Underneath the roughness of his exasperation, William felt the kindness of concern. "Can I get you anything? Would you like a cup of wine to steady you? You look as if you've hit rock bottom."

William shook his head. "I don't want to be drinking. If ever there was a moment to think clearly, it has to be this. I think I've shed more tears in this last year than in the whole of the rest of my life put together. I don't know what it is about this place."

"Really? You don't know what it is?" John's eyes bored into him, challenging him to a better honesty than that.

"'Tis Jesus," William mumbled in answer. "'Tis the Spirit of Jesus."

"Yes! That's what I think too. And you're sure you want to throw that away? You're sure the privilege of being part of what we're doing here doesn't matter to you? William, do you really want this? Look at yourself! Tears pouring down your face—by'r Lady you look as if you'd just lost everything! Are you quite sure you want to go? It isn't that you've made a promise you didn't mean and feel you can't back out of it now?"

William shook his head no. "John, words aren't enough to tell you how I feel about Madeleine. She completes me. She makes sense of my life." He took a deep breath and managed to steady his voice. "It's been a long time finding it, but I feel as though this is what I came here to do. The love between us has been like the first wick green shoots of dog's mercury in the hedgerow at the end of a long winter—a flash of new life when everything else is sere and drab. It's not about excitement or satisfying a lust of the body; it's about being able to be who I was meant to be and trusting someone enough to let her see who I am without being afraid. Well—not very afraid. She gets behind my defenses, without even trying. She just sees me."

John listened intently, his face serious and thoughtful, saying after a while, when William had blown his nose and dried the tears from his face, "I suppose I should be grateful there is someone to take care of my sister, one who loves her that much. I thought it was enough for her to be safe here, but I should have seen more, I suppose. If celibacy is not a calling, it can be a terrible deprivation. To live alone, without the companionship of marriage, family, or community, is a hard sentence for someone who is not called to it. Some people are not whole without a life partner. I think I would not be whole without the community. Vocation encompasses your whole life. It's about what completes you. And you and Madeleine—you think you complete each other?"

William nodded. "Almost. Not quite. It's not complete without your forgiveness, John. And I . . . we shall be living only ten miles down the road. I would have liked to come to Mass here, or to Vespers sometimes, but . . . would it—would I—be welcome?"

John sighed deeply and shut his eyes. "Dear heaven; you do push it, don't you! Anyway, I thought I *had* forgiven you."

"You embraced me with courage. I appreciate that more than I can say. But you and Madeleine—I love you both. It tears me apart to have to choose. Leaving here feels like being skinned alive; that's bad enough by itself. But the idea of the door of your heart shutting behind me as I go . . ."

He shook his head, the words trailing away into silence, his face crumpling again.

John looked at him. "You know, you still remind me of Peregrine. You've got the same awful nose to get at the truth of a thing where any sensibly cautious individual would just leave it and let it work its own way through. He was *just* the same. Well, here it is then. We are friends, you and I. You might think I have forgotten who upheld me and went with me through my own bitter valley. It's not uppermost in my mind at the present time, but I have not forgotten. There is a bond. We are friends. And that is Christ's gift; it is a sacramental thing. These odd circumstances where soul touches soul are Eucharistic. Christ whispers, *Remember me*, and in these encounters where two people bring who they really are to meet in defenseless honesty, his real presence is found. It is a Eucharist, Christ's kiss.

"What about you anyway? Have *you* forgiven *me*? You have begged me for my forgiveness, but I think you must have had some hard thoughts about me pass through your mind in this long desert you've been walking—forbidden to see Madeleine, forbidden to let your bond with me grow into a friendship that would exclude others. Am I forgiven too?"

William was shaking his head. "No. That's not how it is. I honor you for your strength of purpose and for standing back enough to see when things are off balance. And for trusting me to keep to my word that I would stay clear of Madeleine. I have nothing to forgive. I love you, John."

Intrigued, John looked at him. "Do you know, nobody but

you has ever said that to me in my whole life—with the possible exception of my mother. How strange. Thank you, William. Thank you very much. One more thing then. You have never lived with women, have you? I think you had no brothers and sisters—am I right?"

William nodded in affirmation.

"And you have lived the whole of your life from the end of your boyhood in a community of men. William, it's different living with women. Are you sure you're ready for it? Women are not the same as we are. I may have lived here for all my adult life, but I've certainly not forgotten what living with my mother and my sister was like. And you may take it from me that however dear they may be to you, women are surely not easy to live with. A man may do his level best to please them, and he still won't get it right. They ask you to make a stew and you set to it—and then they taste it and say, '*What* did you season this with? Oh.' And they smile, and you can see you got it wrong. And you go to the market for them and toil up the hill with a great basket of provisions and they go through it all while you stand and watch—and every time they look surprised and a bit put out. You got the wrong kind, the wrong size, the wrong amount; it's always the same! And women—intelligent women—can somehow never let anything go. You have an argument, and past sundown you'll be hearing reasons why she's right and you're not. You upset her and have to stand and hear a recital of every character flaw you have and that you're always like this. At the end of every spat you feel chastened and ashamed and wonder how they can put up with you in the noble and long-suffering way they do. The marriage bed may look attractive from the cloister, but monastic life looks like heaven sometimes to a married man. Are you *sure* this is what you want? I tell you now, you fall out with Madeleine and she won't kneel and kiss the ground and beg your forgiveness— more likely she'll slap your face!"

As William listened to John, the practical words of ordinary domesticity steadied him.

"I do hear you," he said in reply. "I have no doubt in my mind that adjusting to this will take everything I have. For sure we shall have our misunderstandings and find ourselves glaring at each other and hating each other and thinking we must have been mad to take each other on. I can see that coming and I'm not looking forward to it, but . . . Yes, to be candid with you, I'm terrified, but . . . I feel embarrassed saying this, it's not really my way of talking, but she is my destiny, John. She has my heart. There has been so much in my life . . . you know most of it, but not all. So much that I've been ashamed of or afraid of. It's damaged me, all of it—I thought, beyond repair. But when I am with her, something in me wakes up; it's as though I remember the man—and even the boy—I was meant to be."

Looking at him, thoughtfully, considering, John believed him. There was no more to be said.

"Well, then—are you composed? Shall we go? In answer to your question about chapel, I should strongly advise you to stick to Holy Redeemer for a year; after that you can come to us if you want, for Vespers, but only for Mass if you do not receive the sacrament—because I cannot dispense you from your vows, and that puts me in an impossible position pastorally if you marry. At Holy Redeemer, my counsel to you is simply not to discuss your history with the priest. He does not know you. Then what you choose to do at Mass will be between you and God. And I shall not forget your offer about accounts, and on our previous record I imagine I'll be glad to take you up on it. And—yes, you are forgiven. In fact—" he hesitated, unsure if he ought to say this, but decided he'd stepped so far beyond how he, as William's abbot, should have handled this that it no longer made much difference. "I'll be proud to have you as a brother-in-law. So, shall we go and find you some secular garb while they're saying Sext and eating lunch?"

The bell was ringing for the midday office as they walked across to the almonry rooms in the gatehouse. William knew exactly what was there because he had examined, valued, and catalogued it all. He found himself some sober, decent clothes—"Keep your shoes," said John—and a cap to cover his tonsured head.

He stripped himself of Peregrine's habit, folded it up, looked at it for a moment, and then kissed it. "Good-bye, my beloved enemy," he said. "I didn't stay long enough to wear out your shelter and your embrace—maybe I never could have." He gave the habit into John's hands. "Such curious legacies," he said. "Columba left me love, and Ellen Cottingham left me freedom."

"Don't forget," said John quietly, "that Christ has left you his peace as well, not as the world gives; he makes his own gifts, and he said with that gift there is no need to be afraid. Oh, I'm sorry—I'm starting to talk in homilies the whole of the time. Look, obviously you won't be needing his habit, but do you want to keep Peregrine's belt? As a keepsake."

He pulled it free of the bundle William had handed him, held it out, and William accepted it with delight.

"Now then . . . here's your money. Be on your way. Don't delude yourself for a minute you will be forgotten. We shan't speak of you—you know the custom—but how could anybody not remember you? Oh—you can have your horse back, too. You brought her; she's yours."

It was a valuable gift, worth a year's salary for a working man, and William was grateful indeed, especially to have his own palfrey—for they knew each other's ways, and the familiarity was comforting. The two men went together to the stables. William saddled up his palfrey and swung up easily into the saddle.

"Are you in one piece?" John asked, squinting up at him, his eyes against the light.

"A bit shaky, but this is the right course," William replied.

John nodded. "I shall be praying for you. I shall keep you both in my prayers." He watched as the palfrey responded to her master's touch, and they began to move off under the gate-house arch. "Oh—William!"

William reined the horse in and looked back, eyebrows raised in inquiry. He had mastered himself and managed to restore a veneer of complete composure. His vulnerable soul had been furled back out of sight. John stood looking up at him, the folded habit held in his arms. "Have you anywhere to stay but this house of Madeleine's?"

William shook his head.

"Then you should be wed. I will obtain permission from the priest of Holy Redeemer to come to the lych-gate there and consecrate your marriage this coming Saturday two hours after noon, if you wish it. I am empowered to write the license; you can do this quietly and without waiting for banns to be read. If we do the thing thus discreetly, I think no one will be asking questions. You will be a married couple, that's all. You have been known as a man in orders in the religious houses, true enough—but as a layman, I doubt you will be recognized."

"You would do that? You would consecrate our marriage yourself? Oh, God bless you! God reward you!" The smile that lit up William's face shone with such sudden radiance that John was quite taken aback. "Till Saturday then; we shall be there!"

John felt glad to his core that he'd found the grace to make the journey it took to release such a dazzle of joy. He held open the gate for his friend to ride out and fastened it behind him. As he turned to go back to his house, listening to the hooves of William's palfrey striking the stones of the road beyond the gate, the sound carrying in the clear, cold winter air, he reflected soberly on how burdened William must have been for most of the time, that he had never even guessed he had the capacity for such a shining radiance of joy.

And so it was that William rode out of St. Alcuin's in peace, comforted—his heart light, eager to find Madeleine, and to see the place that would be their home. And his happiness was John's gift to him. Without that willingness to understand and forgive, he knew he would have been stumbling away free, but wretched and broken.

Within the walls of the abbey, John walked back slowly to his lodging. Once inside, he went into the inner chamber and sat down on his bed, still with the habit that had been Peregrine's and William's held tight in his arms. He needed to be alone for a little while.

He sat quietly, his eyes fixed steadily on the crucifix hanging from its nail in the wall of his chamber, opening his heart to Christ in stunned confession of what he had done. He knew that as the abbot of a religious community, he had transgressed in condoning this marriage—and worse, in offering to consecrate it. He knew his tradition demanded that he dismiss William coldly, reminding him that his solemn profession was irrevocable, that his vows were binding unto death. He knew that in showing him the pathway forward—to marry Madeleine without seeking permission or dispensation, and in so doing create a suspension of the active state of his vow—he had himself committed a grave offense. He should make a clean breast of any sin he committed either to his brethren in chapter or to his confessor—his prior, Father Chad. John ran through the scenario of kneeling to inform the community that he had just blessed William on his way to marry Madeleine, and in addition offered to consecrate the marriage, and rejected it as a possibility. He could not even contemplate telling Father Chad. He wondered if he might make his confession to Father Theodore.

He sat thinking about the influence we have, each one of us upon the other. He faced the reality that the piece of casuistry he was presently engaged on was entirely consistent with William's character and not at all with his own. But nor had William left his mark without being changed himself. The honest repentance, the tears of sorrow, the agony of love that had worked their way into his heart, he had found in this place; the months he had stayed under its shelter had transformed him.

John accepted that somewhere the rule book had got thrown out of the window, but he believed in spite of that they had managed to hang onto the Rule. And he couldn't make proper sense of that, but he felt sure it was true.

He bent his head to rest his cheek on Peregrine's habit, still clasped to his breast. "What would you have done?" he whispered, "what would you have done?"

Thinking about it, he acknowledged that Peregrine would probably not have budged an inch to condone what William was doing. He would certainly have made no plans to be consecrating his marriage. Even so, the conviction persisted that he had done the right thing in forgiving him, in being willing to bless their new beginning.

He kissed the habit he held in his arms and laid it down on his bed. Resolutely he went out of his lodge into the cloister and up the stairs to the novitiate, where he found Theodore going through some difficult Latin with Brother Robert.

"Father, I need to speak with you," he said abruptly. While he waited as Theo quietly arranged to see Robert later, John thought he'd better try very hard after this to get his life back on track. Using his position as abbot to disturb an obedientiary's fulfillment of his vocation was not an exemplary way to be spending the afternoon. Darting a worried look at him, Brother Robert hurried away.

"Who's in trouble?" asked Theo with a smile once they were alone, "you or me?"

He listened carefully as John poured out to him all that had happened; he confessed how, though he had acted with integrity until today, he had wobbled at the last and sent William away with the kiss of peace, advice to get married quietly, and a promise to be the celebrant of that marriage, under license discreetly obtained. He felt guilty, and less certain of the rightness of his course, as he told the tale.

"Is that all?" asked Theo gently when he had finished. "Yes," said John, "that's all. I need your counsel, brother."

Theo thought quietly for several minutes. "Well," he said then, "I do see what you mean. You have bent the rules into some very interesting shapes, my father. But then again, God sent his Son into the world not to condemn the world, but so that through him the world might be saved. Salvation tangles with the human, gets its hands dirty. Condemnation never does. And I guess that's the difference."

✠   ✠   ✠

He did not need to look at the letter again. He had remembered precisely the directions Madeleine had sent him to find their house. It lay just over ten miles south of St. Alcuin's, on the outskirts of the village. Low Street, then Bakehouse Lane, then a left turn by the great oak tree where the road divided, then about a quarter of a mile after that, a low stone wall and a wooden barred gate. The trees intertwined their fingers over the lane. Mud laced hard by frost lay underfoot. Scarlet berries brightened the dark of evergreens and flamed among the yellow of a few last pointed leaves. The dead broken stalks of nettles and cow parsley poked from the long, dying grass at the edges of the way. On the gray stone of walls, lichens and mosses shone in vivid patches of color. Clear of cloud, on this noon all the world was alight with the bright cold of winter. There would be a hard frost again tonight.

William found the place, dismounted, opened the gate, and led his horse in after him—being careful to latch the gate again;

he didn't know what arrangements Madeleine had for her goat here.

He stood gazing in astonished delight at his new home. "A cottage," Thomas Haydon had said, which could have meant anything. William feasted his eyes on this low, comfortable house with a porch to the wide front door, weathered oak under a great stone lintel. A rose that had been trained to grow on the wall now hung loose in long sprays where the care of it had been neglected, only a leaf or two and three lingering blossoms left on it this late in the year. He had not known what to expect but had not anticipated something of such good size. At the front of the house where he stood, the stone-flagged yard adrift with leaves was bounded by a wall. Through the archway in the section of wall opposite him he saw a garden—clearly itself walled, so presumably for vegetables even though at present it looked on a glance to be no more than a haven for weeds.

"Oh! Oh! You have your palfrey! And we have a stable!" An excited Madeleine appeared around the side of the house, where another way through led to the ground at the back. He had sent word to her that he would come today, and she had been listening for the sound of a cart or a horse or even the simple sound of the gate latch as a man came in on foot, every hour of the morning. "Come! Come and see!"

He led his horse through like a man in a dream, to where she had prepared the stable with bedding on the floor, a pail of water, and a net of hay. "I've had the goat in here at night. I didn't know we'd have the palfrey."

"John said I could bring her. She'd come with me from St. Dunstan's."

They fastened her in the stable. "There's a paddock where she can go," said Madeleine, "and we have an orchard, and a pond—we shall be able to have ducks as well as geese, and a pig right away because the orchard is walled and has a pig house at the back. Oh—there is a fruit store by the vegetable garden, all fitted with racks and some apples already laid away. And the wood store is stocked—the wood is well seasoned too! Come and see!"

William followed her in silence, taking in everything she showed him. "Isn't it wonderful? Don't you love it?" She looked for his approval as he stood under the boughs of an apple tree still bearing the last remains of unpicked fruit. She could not read his face. "You—you do like it, don't you?"

He nodded without speaking and hastily wiped a tear from his eye with the heel of his hand.

"I can't believe this kindness from someone we hardly knew." His voice shook as he answered her. "This is a palace. It's so much more than I imagined. I've been afraid for what we would do to provide for ourselves, but you're right—there's room for a pig and geese and ducks and vegetables and all we could need." He smiled at her, trying to get a grip on his tangled emotions. "Where have your hens gone?"

"Over there, look—tucked into the bottom corner of the orchard. There was a henhouse already."

She looked at him, her eyes dancing with joy, and she wrapped her arms about him. "And now there is you, to make it heaven."

And then he bent his face to hers, folded her in his embrace, his mouth joining to hers as he gave himself to the sweetness of their kiss.

"We are home," he said softly, when he could bear to let that kiss come to an end. "It came true."

He cradled her in his arms, drinking in everything about this moment, every nerve awake to the feeling of her body against his, hardly able to take in that this was their home; they could stay. It was given.

"Come and see inside the house! Come and see!" She looked up at him, sparkling with happiness.

"Just a minute," he said, unwilling to let her go, and though he felt her taut with impatience to show him everything, he kissed her again. Then he was ready to look at their house.

The front door opened into a generous room, one wall taken up with the inglenook and bread oven, but there were other rooms besides: the kitchen, of course, and a scullery with a stone sink. From the scullery a door led into a cobbled yard with a well in which Madeleine had found gaps built into the stones to house her butter. Another door opened from the scullery into a pantry with stone shelves and only one small window, built on the north side of the house to keep fresh food cool. A brace of grouse hung there. "Our neighbor brought them," said Madeleine happily, "for a welcome gift." Besides this, the house had three further rooms downstairs, so far bare and empty. "For accounts and deeds and records." "For drying herbs and preparing medicines—a real apothecary." "For a little oratory— one where I'm actually *allowed* to kiss my lady."

The stairs led to an upper floor with four fair-sized rooms. "If we need more money, we could have a lodger—maybe two!" said Madeleine.

"We could," William agreed, but she heard reluctance in his voice. "For a while—only a while—can we be private here? Can it be just you and me for a little while?"

"For sure. Anyway, we have an income as well as a house. I have eight pounds a year, and if I marry, there is ten pounds a year for my spouse, remember. If I never marry, that second amount is to be held in trust and goes to the abbey on my death."

William had remembered. No detail of that will had escaped him, and he had fully grasped the information and its implications on first hearing.

It was a modest income, but with no rent to pay and the possibility of their own meat and eggs and milk, and with a horse already given, they would have to be frugal, but not anxious. The house had still a few sticks of furniture—a bedstead and a large chest with a domed lid in one room upstairs, a

table and two stools, three pails, and some kitchen parapher-
nalia downstairs. "And it was so good of Adam to let me bring
all that I had in the cottage, even though it wasn't mine to
begin with!" *Who?* wondered William momentarily; he could
not get used to Madeleine referring to John always by his
baptismal name.

"We haven't a proper mattress, but I've made one from
bracken and heather from the moor for now," said Madeleine
as they came into the only furnished bedroom. "But Adam said
I could bring the sheepskins. I haven't purchased much, but I
did buy the linen to make the mattress, and two sheets and a
blanket. I got the best price I could, but it was a lot—I hope you
don't think I've been extravagant." She looked at him anxiously.

He smiled at her and kissed her cheek. "What else could you
do? We can make shift with heather and bracken very well, as
you say, for now. Once we have the birds, we can save the feathers until we have enough for a mattress."

"William . . . " She hesitated. "What are we—when are we—
do you know—when will we be able to be wed?"

He raised his eyebrows, and his gaze held hers, teasing.
"Wed? Were you thinking we would be wed?"

But he dropped a kiss on her brow before she could enter-
tain any serious doubt of his intentions. "Nay, if you will have
me, my lady, your good brother has been more generous than
I could ever have expected. He will marry us with a license
to waive the need for banns—this coming Saturday, in the
afternoon, he said. We are to meet him at the lych-gate of Holy
Redeemer."

✠　　✠　　✠

"Brother Conradus."

The novices had finished their lessons for the morning,
stacked the Gospels and the various texts of the Desert Fathers

away neatly on the shelves, and begun to make their way down to chapel for the midday office. Conradus sometimes helped in the kitchen in the mornings too, but Father Theodore remained firm upon the point that he did actually have to learn something sometimes, and he had been in the novitiate schoolroom all this morning. On his way to the door with the others, standing back to make room for Brother Benedict to go ahead of him, he turned in response to his novice master quietly speaking his name.

"Yes, Father?"

"Will you wait just a moment. I wanted to ask you something."

Conradus came back to where Theodore still sat in his place in their circle, watching the young men filter out of the room. He always prayed for each one as they went through the door.

"Come and sit down. I won't keep you but a minute."

Conradus sat beside him, and his novice master waited peacefully until all the others had gone. Brother Robert, the last out, looked back questioningly: should he close the door? And Theodore nodded—yes, please—so he latched it quietly behind him.

"What's the matter, Brother Conradus?" asked Theodore then.

Brother Conradus looked instantly alarmed. "I'm sorry!" he said quickly. "Have I been remiss? Was I looking sullen?"

Theodore smiled. Sometimes it hurt Conradus that almost everything he said seemed to make people laugh, even when he was in earnest, when he was telling them the most heartfelt truth. He comforted himself with the reminder that those who afford others a reason for laughter, who are somehow of themselves a kind of joke, are part of the leaven of righteousness that keeps life from getting heavy and sad. But he couldn't see why his reply had caused his novice master amusement.

"You have not behaved badly, Brother Conradus. You just

look a bit glum—and cheerful is your normal mode of being. What's wrong?"

Conradus sighed. He looked perplexed now. "The thing is, I don't know if I'm allowed to say this, Father."

"You probably are. I am your novice master and your confessor. You can say what you like."

"Well, then, it's Father William. I knew he was unhappy—really unhappy. I told Father John he was. There was a day during the summer when I accidentally came upon him up in the wood. He'd gone there to find some privacy, I suppose, and I'd gone up just for a stroll. And when I found him there, he was crouched on the ground weeping—really sobbing. He was angry to be disturbed and had a few choice words to say to me—he came to find me later and apologized to me—but I could never put it out of my mind after that. He was so very unhappy. I prayed for him every day, and not knowing what to pray for I asked Our Lady for help. And—I told Father Abbot this—the words came into my mind to pray that he would have the courage to keep the flower of his love alive through this winter, for it would have its time in the sun. So that is what I have prayed for, day after day after day. But he never looked any happier, and now I see he has gone. I know I can't ask; I'm not prying. I just feel so sad and disappointed that my prayers were never answered. He gave up without ever getting past December; he didn't struggle through the winter to see that time in the sun."

Theodore digested this in silence, wondering how much, if anything, he could say.

"I'm sorry, Father," said Conradus. "I do know I'm not supposed to mention him."

"This is difficult," Theodore said slowly, "but I can tell you this much: your prayers have not gone unanswered. He had the courage. He kept it alive. It has its time in the sun. You can give thanks. And he would be touched and grateful to know you had prayed so faithfully, for it was very hard going for him at times. That's all I can say to you, apart from that it's worth bearing in mind that many of our prayers are answered beyond the horizon of our sight—but that's a limitation of what we can see, not the failure of our faith or our prayer."

"He's—he's all right then?" Theo watched the young man's eyes brighten with hope and relief.

"I believe so," said Theodore. "I really cannot tell you anything more than that."

"But we've only this week begun Advent. We haven't gone through the winter."

Theodore looked at him with a certain amount of wonder. The realm of thought and philosophy was his natural medium, and it never failed to surprise him how opaque that realm could be to the literal minded.

"I think," he said, "Our Lady may have been speaking figuratively."

✠   ✠   ✠

"Sweetheart; we are man and wife now. We are safe in the privacy of our own chamber. Here I am, in my own skin. I know it's chill, but might you not think of removing your shift? I give you my word, I'll keep you warm!"

Madeleine, sitting on the edge of the bed brushing her hair far more thoroughly and for longer than was necessary, paused and looked round at him.

"To be honest with you, I'm shy," she admitted in a small voice. "I've never done this before. And I think if I still had the body of a girl I'd be proud and excited, but . . . "

"Yes?" he prompted her softly.

"I am a mature woman, William. I am no longer beautiful."

He moved across the bed and knelt behind her, put his arms

around her, buried his face in the heavy fall of her dark hair streaked with silver, pushed it aside, and kissed her neck.

"Will you let me be the judge of that? Will being beautiful to me be beautiful enough? And can I ask you, am I beautiful to you?"

She twisted around toward him, hasty to reassure.

"You are! You are lovely. Every inch of you."

"Well, shall I tell you something? A month or so back your good brother told me I am nothing but a bundle of bones. He said my face looks hard and drawn and lined. Desperate, he said. He told me I'd aged and had a grim, dusty look to me. He said the whole light about me is gray, whatever he meant by that. And he concluded by telling me my eyes are red and that's the only color left in me. Now, my best beloved, what do you think I felt?"

"Hurt, I should think. It doesn't sound very kind."

"John is always kind. He was trying to make me eat and rest more. And no, I didn't feel hurt, I felt terrified—so frightened I felt sick, lest the day should come when you and I had our chance, and you looked at me and didn't want me anymore. And do you want me?"

"Oh, my sweetheart!"

She scrambled up onto the bed to hold him in her arms. "Of course I want you! You are beautiful. You are adorable."

"Well, I am also the man your brother described. So even if under that nightdress you have the body of a woman of ninety, we shall be a good match. Therefore, of your charity, will you not take it off? Look, we have only the remains of the fire and one candle burning here. It's a kindly light, but if you want I can blow the candle out, and we will make love by starlight and ember glow."

Madeleine hesitated still. "Yes," she said, "will you do that?"

So he crawled across and took his time blowing out the candle that stood on the chest beside the head of the bed, and when he turned back, she knelt shy on the bed, dressed in only her long fall of silver-streaked dark hair, mysterious and lovely in the moonlight.

"Oh, my dear!" he whispered and held out his arms to her, and she crept into his embrace.

He held her tenderly, feeling her tension. "Are you afraid?" he asked her, his lips leaving light kisses on her brow.

"Awkward, more," she said. "I am not used to this intimacy."

"Nay; well, there wasn't much of it in a monastery either. We can get over that. The time will come when we are just easy with each other, but there is no way to arrive there without getting used to one another—there has to be a first time. I am more concerned that you have been hurt, you have been violated, and I think you might be afraid. So I want you to know—" like a constellation of stars barely there in the evening sky, she felt his kisses on her cheek, her throat, her ear "—that it will always be gentle with me; never rough, never demanding. And if you say 'stop,' then we stop."

And he held her quietly, waiting for her response. "I am not afraid," she said. "I feel that I can trust you absolutely. I believe that you love me. And though I have lost all the beauty of my youth, for some reason I cannot fathom you do seem to find me desirable."

She felt his lips curve in a smile against her cheek. "Well . . . as to that," he murmured, "I don't wish to be too cocky in my presumption, but I've a cheery hope rising that all will be well. Come, my love, believe in this. Believe in us."

And in the beautiful rhythms of tenderness and trust, letting defenses melt away, finding delight and, deeper, discovering exquisite pleasure in surrender to this love that finally had its day, they consummated their marriage. Patient and tender. Light and slow.

Their bodies entwined together, folded in the peaceful,

grateful afterglow of love, all hunger satisfied, they fell asleep. And the stars watched over them, and the silver moon.

✠   ✠   ✠

"D' you miss William?"

This sudden question came from Brother Thomas, who had lit the fire for his abbot on this dismal, freezing day between Christmas and the new year and now sat in one of the chairs at the hearthside, a capacious cloth spread over his lap, rubbing grease into John's boots.

Abbot John did not respond immediately, but the stillness Tom's words brought signaled that he had heard. John frowned. When a man left the community, he was not discussed. His name was never mentioned again. That was the custom. Tom knew that.

For a moment, John considered simply not replying and leaving the matter to the tradition of silence. But on consideration he recognized that he and Tom and William had formed a strange triangle—William's unexpected arrival, complete with a personality it was impossible to accommodate in any kind of tranquil manner, had got between the abbot and his esquire. John thought on reflection that the question was fair and needed to be asked. So he looked up from the preparation for his catechetics class. Tom was not waiting for an answer; he was calmly continuing to polish the boots.

"Assuredly I miss him," said John. "No dramas in Chapter. No hangings. No illicit love affairs. No shipwrecks. No sudden reversals of fortune. The place isn't the same without him."

Tom smiled. "Yes. He shook us up a bit. He didn't belong here. I think the abbey spat him out something like the whale spat Jonah out. He gave the whole building a bellyache. But it wasn't a waste of time, was it? I learned to see him differently—all of what happened while he was here taught me that you can't always tell; there are two sides to everything, and people aren't always what they seem. I try to remember that now in my dealings with everyone. Even when someone seems completely bloody minded and I'm losing my patience fast. I think back to the way William behaved toward Father Peregrine and then where we got to in the end, and I don't give up on the men I can't see eye to eye with, as once I might have done. He found out who he was, too, didn't he? He was called to be a householder—a married man—not a monk. I'm assuming he went with Madeleine. It was clear enough to see he was head over heels in love with her when you brought her back here. And I'm guessing—stop me if this is impertinent and not welcome—that you put a stop to that, because something was snuffed out in him in midsummer. When you came back with Oswald, he was luminous. I don't know what happened there. But in Madeleine's company, he was different again—he was . . . purely happy, I think. Not a holy thing; just ordinary human happiness, something he wanted and couldn't help reaching out for. I felt so sorry for him at the time because it could obviously only end in tears, in short order too, and so it did. And since then all the light, all the happiness, they've been gone. He looked more haunted every day. If he had a chance to find that happiness he lost, well, God bless him. You can't be in community if it's become a living purgatory for you."

He put the boot down and picked up the other one. "Is this all right? Am I speaking out of turn?"

He glanced up at his abbot, who was listening to him quietly.

"Yes, you are, and you know it; but yes, it's all right," said John. "Speaking out of turn is how I know it's you."

Tom smiled. "Yes. When William asked me to teach him how to love, I asked him in return to teach me to think before I speak, and he said he thought that would be impossible. You know, I'm glad he came. I'm glad we had this time. He did learn how to love, albeit not quite what we had in mind. But it wasn't only Madeleine; he loved us too—loved the whole place, even the wood and the stones and the store chests—perhaps especially those! He loved you, Father. He was devoted to you. I'm guessing it must have been a hard choice to leave, even for Madeleine."

"Not a hard choice, I think," said John thoughtfully. "Not really a choice at all. She had his heart, and a man has to be where his heart is. But he said it felt like being skinned alive to leave us."

"Did he?" Tom chuckled. "That's my lad: understated and sanguine to the last!"

He set down the greasy cloth and picked up the dry one for buffing.

"Well, I think for all it was a bit like lightning making a direct hit on the house—we learned a lot, and so did he. I'm glad we had Oswald here too, and that he knew some comfort and kindness for a while—besides, I'd never realized before what an important organ the tongue is! I assumed it was just for speaking—never gave it a moment's thought beyond that. I never knew a man would die without his tongue. And I'm glad Madeleine came—that she had a chance at having a man of her own and being a married woman—and that some healing came there, for those terrible things that befell her and your mother. And if your mother still watches over us, I'll wager she had a hand in that healing. I'm glad about the shipwreck, too. I reckon it taught William that all the tricksy, clever dodges he set so much store by are not to be trusted, and they are neither the way of Christ nor the way of well-being. It's Mammon, all that wheeling and dealing. The ways of Christ are open and simple. And again and again he learned here that nobody can earn love, forgiveness, understanding; those are gifts, it's in their nature to be freely given. It cost him dear, learning that. He's never got rid of the tic in his face that began the day he had to come and tell us in Chapter about the money. Had it ever since."

He swapped the boots again and began buffing the second one.

"I've taken a lot of lessons from this time. One of the things I've had to learn is that I couldn't be possessive about you—but that didn't cut into me as deep as the same lesson cut into him. He got very close to you, didn't he? And I'm guessing you put a stop to that too, and that hurt him badly. Only guessing, but . . . anyway . . . there wasn't a day passed without something that hurt him or was taken away from him, or that he had to accept he'd got all wrong—except when he was crossing all the boundaries and making up a new Rule of his own. He was not made for community, that man. But, Father—" Tom put down the boot, finished, alongside its mate, and looked up at his abbot "—I hope you will permit him still to be our friend."

John lifted his eyebrows. "Did he speak to you about that?"

"No. He never spoke to any of us about anything, as far as I know. Most of what we know about William was by conjecture. I think he only ever talked to you."

John nodded. "Well, he did ask if he might come here to church and if we could stay friends. I was feeling a bit raw at the time, and in any case I think there has to be a space. In a year, I said, he could come back to us for Mass, provided he accepts he can't receive the Sacrament. And I shall see them— Madeleine is my sister, after all. I . . . I don't know if I should be telling you this, but I will. I married them two weeks ago. They seemed very happy."

Tom smiled. *"Christus victor,"* he said. "Here's your boots, Father."

✠　　✠　　✠

It was very cold, with the fire out, when the sun came up that winter morning. Frost flowers jostled thick on the window glass. William felt profoundly grateful the house had been kept

211

up to date and at some point the windows had been glazed. Madeleine lay fast asleep still, but he, attuned to monastic hours, had lain awake some time. He didn't move. He didn't want to wake her. In the abbey they would just about be finishing Lauds now, probably, he thought. He prayed in thanksgiving and consecration for this new day, and he smelt the frost in the air. His breath hung as cloudy as smoke when he exhaled. He turned his head and, for a while, looked at Madeleine's tumbled hair and features quiet in sleep. He thought he could see different things in her while she was sleeping, and that interested him.

He liked the silence of this house empty of all but the two of them. He thought silence was something like water, the place where things—the words of God maybe—could at last become clear.

He looked at the gradual dove colors of dawn leavening the darkness of their chamber, and he watched the rising sun fill the room with light. He reflected that, for the first time in his whole life he could ever remember, he felt free of wretched guilt. The perpetual hunger and restlessness at the core of him had been brought to peace, as though he had been healed of a wound he had only half known was there, had been made whole. He just felt peaceful, everything in him satisfied. No despair. Nothing to hide and lie about. No horrible sick feeling in the pit of his stomach. Even the persistent tic in his face had gone away. The struggle he'd been through had about torn him apart, but this morning he knew that he had been put back together again—"re-membered," as John had said. And he didn't feel afraid anymore.

GLOSSARY OF TERMS

Ambulatory: a passage curving round from behind the choir and its sanctuary, linking the north and south transepts and giving access to various small side chapels and the sacristy.

Cardinal office: Lauds and Vespers are the cardinal offices of the monastic day. The word *cardinal* comes from the Latin word *cardo*, meaning "hinge," for these offices open and close the day.

Cellarer: monk responsible for oversight of all provisions; a key role in the community.

Chapter: daily meeting governing practical matters, where a chapter of St. Benedict's Rule was read and expounded by the abbot.

Checker: a small, separate building, in the part of the monastery accessible to laypeople, where all the documents of trade (receipts, account books, etc.) were kept, and where tradespeople could be received. The word *exchequer* comes from this.

Choir: the part of the church where the community sits.

Cloister: covered way giving access to main buildings of a monastery.

Cordwainer: leatherworker.

Corrody: purchased right to food/clothing/housing from a monastery for an agreed period, which could be for life.

Dorter: sleeping quarters.

Frater: refectory.

Grand Silence: The silence kept by the whole community from after Compline when they retired for the night until after first Mass in the morning.

Keeping custody of the eyes: refraining from looking around.

Morrow Mass: the first of two daily celebrations of the Mass, this one being smaller and more intimate than the later one open to the wider public.

Mortifying his eyes: looking down, not glancing about.

Nave: the body of the church occupied by the public in worship.

Nipperkin (or pipkin): very small liquid measure (no longer in common use), less than a fluid ounce—perhaps about 25 milliliters.

Night stairs: from the sleeping quarters of a monastery, a staircase led down directly into the church to allow easy access for the devotions taking place in the middle of every night.

Obedientiary: monk assigned to a specific role in his community.

Office: the set worship taking place at regular intervals through the day.

Palfrey: high-bred riding horse.

Postulant: person aspiring to join the community, living in the monastery in the stage of commitment preceding entry into the novitiate.

Transept: area between the apse (the part of the church where the choir and its sanctuary are) and the nave (the main body of the church where the congregation from the parish sits). The south transept and north transept meet in the square "crossing" the junction of all four arms of the cruciform church.

Viaticum: literally, "food for the journey"; name given to the bread and wine of the last rites for the dying.

Warming room: The place in a medieval monastery that served as a common room. It had a big fireplace.

Wes hal: Old English greeting meaning "Be thou whole"; origin of "Hallo/hello/hail!"

Wick: alive; full of vitality.

Monastic Day

There may be slight variation from place to place and at different times from the Dark Ages through the Middle Ages and onward—e.g., Vespers may be after supper rather than before. This gives a rough outline. Slight liberties are taken in my novels to allow human interactions to play out.

Winter Schedule (from Michaelmas)
2:30 a.m. Preparation for the nocturns of matins: psalms, etc.
3:00 a.m. Matins, with prayers for the royal family and for the dead.
5:00 a.m. Reading in preparation for Lauds.
6:00 a.m. Lauds at daybreak and Prime; wash and break fast (just bread and water, standing).
8:30 a.m. Terce, Morrow Mass, Chapter.
12:00 noon Sext, Sung Mass, midday meal.
2:00 p.m. None.
4:15 p.m. Vespers, Supper, Collatio.
6:15 p.m. Compline.
The Grand Silence begins.

Summer Schedule
1:30 a.m. Preparation for the nocturns of matins: psalms, etc.
2:00 a.m. Matins.
3:30 a.m. Lauds at daybreak, wash and break fast.
6:00 a.m. Prime, Morrow Mass, Chapter.
8:00 a.m. Terce, Sung Mass.
11:30 a.m. Sext, midday meal.
2:30 p.m. None.
5:30 p.m. Vespers, Supper, Collatio.
8:00 p.m. Compline.
The Grand Silence begins.

Liturgical Calendar

I have included the main feasts and fasts in the cycle of the church's year, plus one or two other dates that are mentioned (for example, Michaelmas and Lady Day when rents were traditionally collected) in these stories.

Advent: begins four Sundays before Christmas.
Christmas: December 25th.
Holy Innocents: December 28th.
Epiphany: January 6th.
Baptism of our Lord: concludes Christmastide, the Sunday after January 6th.
Candlemas: February 2 (Purification of Blessed Virgin Mary, Presentation of Christ in the temple).
Lent: Ash Wednesday to Holy Thursday; start date varies with phases of the moon.
Holy Week: last week of Lent and the Easter Triduum.
Easter Triduum (three days) of Good Friday, Holy Saturday, Easter Sunday.
Ascension: forty days after Easter.
Whitsun (Pentecost): fifty days after Easter.
Lady Day: May 31st.
Trinity Sunday: Sunday after Pentecost.
Corpus Christi: Thursday after Trinity Sunday.
Sacred Heart of Jesus: Friday of the following week.
Feast of John the Baptist: June 24th.
Lammas (literally "loaf-mass"; grain harvest): August 1st.
Michaelmas: feast of St. Michael and All Angels, September 29th.
All Saints: November 1st.
All Souls: November 2nd.
Martinmas: November 11th.

Also Available in
The Hawk and the Dove series

Books 1-3

Book 4

Book 5